# He turned to leave and stopped in his tracks.

He stared at her, and with his free hand pulled her to him.

He lowered his head, his lips touching hers in a kiss that sent bolts of lightning through her body.

The kiss was gentle, a touching of lips and the gentle probing of his tongue. It was sweet like honey and he wanted to sip like a bee enjoying its first taste of pollen.

When his lips left her, she felt an unexpected sense of disappointment. She instinctively leaned forward, wanting to feel his touch again.

"And you pretend you don't want me," he teased, a big grin on his face. "Sweet dreams. I'll be dreaming of you, too."

With that he turned and walked away, confidence in his swagger.

She touched her lips, still feeling the slight pressure of his.

He was right. She'd be dreaming of him tonight— of him and a sweet, stolen kiss.

**Books by Wayne Jordan**

Kimani Romance

*Embracing the Moonlight*
*One Gentle Knight*
*To Love a Knight*
*Always a Knight*
*Midnight Kisses*
*Saved by Her Embrace*

---

## WAYNE JORDAN

For as long as he can remember, Wayne Jordan loved reading, but he also enjoyed creating his own make-believe worlds. This love for reading and writing continued, and in November 2005 his first book, *Capture the Sunrise,* was published by BET Books.

Wayne has always been an advocate for romance, especially African-American romance. In 1999 he founded www.romanceincolor.com, a website that focuses on African-American romance and its authors.

Wayne is a high school teacher and a graduate of the University of the West Indies. He holds a B.A. in literature and linguistics and an M.A. in applied linguistics. He lives on the beautiful tropical island of Barbados, which, with its white sands and golden sunshine, is the perfect setting for the romance stories he loves to create. Of course, he still takes time out to immerse himself in the latest release from one of his favorite authors.

# Saved
## BY *Her*
# EMBRACE

## WAYNE JORDAN

KIMANI™
ROMANCE

To the authors who have, over the years, inspired me...
and encouraged me to *never give up*.

 KIMANI PRESS™

ISBN-13: 978-0-373-86219-1

Recycling programs
for this product may
not exist in your area.

SAVED BY HER EMBRACE

www.kimanipress.com

**Printed in U.S.A.**

Dear Reader

I hope you enjoyed *Saved by Her Embrace*. Shayne's best friends, Troy and George, have always intrigued me, so when readers asked for their stories, I was delighted to oblige. Of course, I couldn't write Dr. Troy's story without pairing him with the doctor-hating, outspoken Sandra Walters. I enjoyed creating their fiery love-hate relationship, but of course they had to realize that they needed each other and there was no running away from true love.

As I write this letter, I'm putting the finishing touches on *Tempted by His Touch*. George Simpson is one of my favorite characters. He's muscular, sexy and cynical about love, but when his childhood sweetheart reenters his life, he realizes that forgiveness is the step he must take to find his happily-ever-after.

I love hearing from my readers. Feel free to email me at authorwj@caribsurf.com or visit my website at www.waynejordan.net.

Thanks for your continued support.

Wayne

# *Prologue*

Sandra hated doctors, but Dr. Troy Whitehall was good on the eyes. He was tall, dark and drop-dead gorgeous! But he was a doctor, and a man of *that* profession was the last person on earth she'd ever get involved with…again.

He was sexy. Though the word *sexy* didn't come close to describing the whole package.

But he was a doctor, and his perfectly toned, muscular, six-pack-abs body would not tempt her from her resolve to stay away.

Today, the wedding of her best friend, Carla, and the man of Carla's dreams, Shayne Knight, would pass and she wouldn't have to see Troy again anytime soon.

Despite his good looks, she found him arrogant and downright obnoxious at times.

He was probably a playa, the love 'em and leave 'em kind. That's how he looked and she was sure that in time she would discover that he was just like that. He was too gorgeous to be the committed kind of individual. He reminded her of her father, Dr. Christopher Walters. Her father was handsome and cocky like Troy and had been committed to his work, or so she thought. Then one day, he'd asked her mother for a divorce, and two days after the divorce had been finalized, he had married a nurse with perfect silicone breasts.

To say that she'd been disappointed would be an understatement. At the time of the divorce, she had already been in her late teens and had hardened her heart to him and moved on. Ten years later, she'd still not said a word to her father. Her mother had not taken it easily, and in time she'd given up on life, passing away, a frail image of her former, vibrant self. Sandra had never forgiven her father.

She glanced around the large tent that had been set up on the grounds of the plantation. Pink and silver hearts decorated the tables, while white balloons hung in clusters like large grapes overhead.

Next to her at the bridal table, Troy laughed, a husky sound that echoed around the room. Female heads turned in his direction, and Sandra could see the eyes of the women devouring him as if he were edible.

She wondered how he'd taste.

*Was she going crazy?* She'd lost perspective for the briefest of moments. Amazing. Men like him worked their magic, and in no time she'd been under his spell. Sandra calmed herself. She would resist.

She glanced across at him, watching his face animated with life.

He was handsome, with a strong face that seemed sculpted by a skilled hand. He wore a neatly trimmed mustache and beard. Short dreadlocks fell to his shoulders, giving him a cavalier look.

His dark mahogany eyes were deep pools that flicked with alertness, only warming when focused on one of his friends. His eyes were filled with intelligence, but guarded.

One thing she could say in his defense was that he seemed like a loyal friend. She could see the affection he had for Shayne and the camaraderie that they shared with their friend George Simpson. George was a man she could handle. A lawyer, he was outspoken, self-assured and loved being the center of attention. But there was an openness about him that was appealing and refreshing.

Her nape tingled and her eyes drifted to Troy. He was looking at her again.

His gaze lingered. Her body tingled, betraying her resolve to ignore the feelings he stirred in her. She blushed, lowering her eyes. She was human, just like the other women, so her being attracted to him was not surprising.

She just had to be strong, but he was making it more and more difficult. Under the table his leg brushed hers for the hundredth time, and she wondered if he was doing it deliberately. She lifted her third glass of wine to her lips, and in an unladylike way, she gulped it down.

She motioned to one of the servers.

Another glass of wine should help her to relax and deal with the sexy bundle of manhood. If she did anything out of the ordinary, she could always blame the wine for her lack of proper judgment.

Dr. Troy Whitehall glanced surreptitiously at the lovely Sandra Walters sitting next to him. Damn, she was beautiful. He'd been mesmerized by her from the moment he'd met her, but for some reason, she just didn't seem to like him. No, that was a bit too mild. She seemed to dislike him intensely. He could see it in the way she tensed whenever he was around and in the looks of disgust whenever she glanced in his direction.

Not to say he blamed her. His flirtation had been a bit heavy-handed. He knew when a woman was attracted to him. He noticed, at times, that her breathing stopped when he was near. He only had to let his gaze linger and caress.

She was sexy. She was definitely the kind of woman he liked bedding. Unfortunately, it wasn't often he had a woman in his bed. These days his focus was on his work and on his dream to be the best neurosurgeon in Barbados.

But he did like the occasional diversion, the occasional fling. He loved sex. Loved the feel of a woman's naked body, hot and sweaty, next to, him or even better, under him. Loved the rush that came with an orgasm that made him scream out loud and shudder with passion.

That's what he was sure it would be like with the sexy Ms. Walters. A curl-your-toes, abs-contracting, shout-out-loud orgasm!

He planned on making his fantasy with Ms. Walters a reality.

Tonight, before the clock struck midnight, he planned to have his Cinderella groaning beneath him. Tomorrow, he would give her back her glass slippers and go back to focusing on what was important…his career.

He watched as Sandra sipped another glass of wine. He reached over and took the glass from her.

"No more for you," he said, placing the glass on the table.

She giggled. "And what do you plan to do about it?" she said, pouting.

"If you're not careful, you're going to find out."

"And what do you plan to do to me if I'm not careful? Spank me?" she asked, giggling and almost knocking her glass over as she reached to take it back.

"I think you've had enough. The others are leaving. I'm taking you to get some fresh air."

"And what if I don't go with you? My mother always told me to beware of the big bad wolf."

"I may be bad at times, but I'm no wolf. I'm definitely a hot-blooded male."

"I can see that. I can feel the heat," she replied. Her boldness surprised him.

"So you're coming with me, or do I have to take you over my shoulders?"

She giggled again but paused, thinking of the choice he'd given her. "I'll come with you," she said hesitantly.

He stood, waiting for her to stand before he shifted her chair.

She followed him reluctantly, so he placed his hand under her elbow and guided her out the door and toward the plantation gardens.

He held her hand while they walked.

A gust of wind startled them briefly and he shivered. A night like this was made for being outdoors, the heat of the day forgotten with the cool Atlantic breeze.

The night was perfect for romance, and he was sure Shayne and Carla would make use of the full moon high above.

In the distance, he could smell the soft fragrance of the island's flowers that grew in the plantation's gardens. So much had changed since Shayne and Carla got together. The once stark, barren grounds had been transformed into a kaleidoscope of color. Pale yellow frangipanis, like the one Sandra wore in her hair, bloomed in abundance. They were favorites of Carla's.

He felt strange and a bit guilty, as if his plan to seduce Sandra was wrong.

When they reached the gardens, he took her over to one of the many benches dotted across the grounds. This one nestled under the canopy of an almond tree.

He waited until she sat before he lowered himself onto the bench.

She was no longer giggling; the cool night air seemed

to have sobered her. Though she wasn't drunk, he could tell that the sweetness of the merlot had lowered her inhibitions.

He glanced at her, the darkness of the trees casting shadows on her face. She was beautiful, her midnight-dark hair cascading to her shoulders. Her lips, perfectly bowed, pouted seductively. He wanted to kiss her.

"So, do you plan on kissing me?" she asked, her lips in a girlish pout.

"You don't mince your words, do you?" he replied. "I was trying to be a gentleman."

"I already know you're not a gentleman, so that's definitely not going to work. But I do want you to kiss me. I've been wondering all evening what it would feel like to be kissed by you." She moved closer to him, her head resting on his shoulder, her lips hovering by his ear.

He turned toward her and lowered his head, capturing her lips with his.

Damn, they were soft and sweet. Lips that tasted like warm honey. He drew her close to him, feeling the firmness of her breasts, and ached to touch her there.

He plunged his tongue inside, loving the soft cooing sound she made in response. She placed her arms around his neck, drawing him closer, as if she wanted him to become a part of her.

His erection strained against his trousers and he wanted nothing more than to strip her naked and bury himself deep inside her warmth.

Her lips left him.

"I want you to make love to me," she said softly, as if

she were not certain she was doing the right thing. For a moment he hesitated, but she placed her hand against his firmness, running her hand along its length.

He groaned as a surge of heat caused his manhood to jerk in response. There was no turning back for him.

It was probably the wedding, the music and the moon. In the morning, he would regret it, but tonight, he wanted to forget everything. His patients, the hospital, his dreams. All he wanted was right here in the form of this hot, sexy woman.

"Come with me," he said. "Your room or mine? We could go to my home. I live just a few miles away."

"My room is closer," she said.

He nodded his head in agreement, stood and then helped her up. He drew her to him, holding her closely until he could feel her heartbeat.

When he released her, he took her hand in his and led her back to the house.

Ten minutes later, he followed Sandra into her room.

Inside, Troy hesitated briefly before he closed the door. The sound of rustling drew him and he watched as she took her clothes off, her eyes focused on him. The brilliant light of the tropical full moon caressed her softly, allowing him to watch her sensual striptease.

God, she was beautiful. He wanted to see her better. He walked over to her, his eyes focused on her nakedness.

He quickly discarded his clothes and stood, naked and erect, before her.

Sandra took a step forward, her hand reaching to grip

his penis. He shuddered with the heat of the contact. He stifled the groan of pleasure building inside.

If he wasn't careful, he'd be embarrassing himself before he made love to her.

He reached for her hand. "No, I'm a bit too excited right now."

She looked down at him. "I definitely don't want this to be over before we begin. I want you to ride me long and hard."

Her response only served to intensify his desire. She removed her hand and rubbed herself against him, moving to some imaginary music, but music he could almost hear in the sway of her body.

He reached down and lifted her to her feet, carrying her to the bed. Laying her gently down, he joined her, careful not to hurt her with his size. At six feet three inches, he was tall, and to him she seemed delicate.

As the moon caressed her, he savored her beauty. She lay on the bed, legs slightly apart. He could tell she was as ready as he was.

But he wanted to pleasure her first. He raised himself above her, wanting to taste more of her honey-dipped lips.

So he kissed her, this time savoring the moment. His mouth moved on hers, tasting and sipping the sweetness there. He moved his mouth downward, blowing gently on one dusky nipple and then the other, watching as she writhed in excitement under him.

She groaned beneath him; her body arched upward, giving him even more access to her nakedness.

His mouth traveled lower, brushing against the soft down covering her womanhood.

His fingers parted her, and he slipped his tongue inside, licking and plunging it in and out of her.

Beneath him, her body shuddered with excitement. It pleased him that she was enjoying it.

He loved her scent, all soft and flowery, like the freshness of a tropical hibiscus.

He paused briefly, remembering that he needed to protect her. He shifted off her, rose from the bed and searched for his pants on the floor. He fumbled in the dim light but found the package of condoms he kept in his back pocket. He carefully opened the package and sheathed himself, aware that she watched his every move.

He joined her on the bed, his excitement heightened by an overwhelming need to be buried inside her. He poised himself above her and entered her slowly. Her body jerked with the power of his entry. He stopped momentarily, feeling the rush of excitement coursing through him.

She was warm and tight, and it took all of his self-control not to give in to the need to go fast and hard. He wanted to revel in the moment, feel the passion that emitted from her.

He eased his hips backward and then forward, stroking her slowly and leisurely. His movement, firm and strong, stoked the fire inside him, and his body reveled in the heat.

He changed pace, moving his hips sideways. Lifting her leg and placing it around his neck, he thrust firmly, deepening his entry until he could feel the complete depth of her womanhood. Beneath him, she groaned, her own hips moving to meet him.

Again he changed position, lying flat upon her while his pelvis moved jerkily, allowing him to pleasure her with short, deep strokes. This allowed his mouth to touch her.

They kissed, deep and long, until he tasted her essence.

And then it happened, a tightening of the muscles in his body and a sweet sensation along the length of his manhood. His body began to shiver wildly.

He continued to stroke her hard, his movements erratic with the anticipation of his release. And then he felt his body explode, the heat rushing through him and from him. Sandra's cry of release came simultaneously as her body shuddered.

He gripped her firmly, drawing her closer, wanting to feel her softness against him, his body contracting with the force of his orgasm. Time passed slowly as his body fluctuated between pleasure and glorious pain.

He shifted from on top of her, knowing that his weight pressed against her. They lay side by side, their bodies facing each other. For a moment, they looked into each other's eyes, cautiously, hesitantly.

In her eyes, Troy saw the same wonder he knew was reflected in his. He wasn't sure what had happened, but it left him feeling strangely vulnerable and exposed.

Something different had happened. And he liked it. He didn't feel like getting up and heading home as he usually did. Instead, he kissed her on the forehead, tasting the salty sweat dotted there.

He didn't know what he was going to do, but thinking of it now was a bit too much effort. He glanced down at her. She was asleep.

He closed his eyes. He was tired. Making love with her was a demanding experience, but one he knew he wanted again. With that he inhaled deeply; the hint of the frangipani she'd worn in her hair still lingered.

He smiled, and the last thing he remembered was that he felt happy.

Sandra woke to the sound of gentle snoring. Where on earth was she? She opened her eyes slowly, allowing them to adjust to the still-dark room. She glanced at the clock on the wall. 5:30 a.m. She didn't want to turn, but the hardness of the body pressed against her brought an image, bold and clear, back to mind.

Oh, my God! What had she done?

Next to her Troy lay asleep, confirming without a doubt that what had transpired was very much a reality.

She shifted into a sitting position, breathing deeply.

She glanced down at the man who lay on the bed next to her.

He was naked, his stomach to the bed, his firm buttocks exposed. She looked around for the covers, finding them and drawing them tightly around her.

Her gaze moved back to Troy.

Her body stirred, his nakedness reminding her of the passion they'd shared the night before.

What was she going to do? she wondered. What had

happened was so out of character for her. She never, ever slept with a man until she knew him well…and liked him.

She wanted to leave, but she needed to wash his scent off her. His scent alone made her act irrationally. She slipped from the bed quietly. She didn't want to wake him. She didn't know how she'd face him, knowing the things he had done to her…and the things she had done to him.

Her face warmed with embarrassment and shame.

It had been so good. So good.

She felt exhausted but in a totally, I've-been-ravished kind of way.

He'd ravished her and she'd enjoyed every moment of it. She'd loved the feel of him deep inside her and the way he moved. One minute he'd entered with long, slow, deep strokes and then he'd changed pace and the ride had turned wild and so, so crazy.

And she'd held on for dear life, meeting him stroke for stroke until she felt that the joy would never end.

But it had.

She turned the shower to cool, needing to rid her body of the heat that made her ache for him.

When she stepped back into the room, she realized that she should have moved earlier. Troy sat at the edge of the bed, the sheet pulled around him.

He glanced up when she walked in, a ready smile on his face, but when he saw her expression, his own changed.

He stood slowly. "So this is when you tell me that it

was all a mistake and it shouldn't have happened," he said, his voice tinged with sarcasm.

She had the grace to blush. Had her regret been so obvious?

"I could say thanks for a good night and have a good life," he continued, dropping the sheet from around him and reaching for his clothes on the floor. She averted her eyes. Even now her body wanted to betray her.

"You're not being reasonable. I probably won't say it's a mistake, but I don't think it should have happened. We were both vulnerable. Good wine, good music, romance and marriage in the air. No wonder we responded as we did."

"That's true," he replied, shrugging indifferently as he pulled his pants on. "Maybe that's what it was."

He put his shirt on and then his shoes without saying anything. The tension in the room sparked.

"I'll head home now. I know when I'm not wanted around. You have a great day. And enjoy your flight back to the U.S." She could tell he was annoyed.

With that, he turned and walked to the door, opened it and left. She expected him to look back, but he didn't.

He'd said all he had to say. She'd not expected such a reaction, but it was for the best.

She quickly dried her skin and tossed on her clothes. Hopefully, no one else in the house was stirring.

Several minutes later, she sat on the bed in her room. She'd get some rest. Maybe that would help her to stop thinking about Troy. Despite her decision, she could not forget the passion they'd shared. But his attitude only proved that she'd made the right decision. She was a consenting adult and had given in to her need for sex. She'd seen an attractive man and wanted him. Pure and simple.

A wave of emotion washed over her and she wondered what it was.

Sadness, she finally admitted.

At unexpected times, she wanted what Carla had. She wanted a good man, a ring on her finger and children, but to dream of that with Troy would be to take fantasy to another level.

Over the years, her luck with men had left her feeling empty and alone. She thought she had finally found her happily-ever-after with the handsome Dr. Peter Drakes, but he'd ruined her dream. Walking into his office at the hospital and finding him humping one of the nurses had forced her to take off the rose-tinted glasses she wore. She'd looked closely at him and seen the image of her father.

She shook her head.

She was being pathetic. There was no sense in dwelling on the impossible. Maybe someday a good man would come along, but it definitely wouldn't be the good Dr. Troy Whitehall!

Troy turned the car on and drove out of the parking area of the plantation yard.

He groaned. The past few days off from work had been good for him. He had needed a break from the hospital, and the rest and relaxation had helped. His mother constantly told him he worked too hard and if he kept it up, she'd never have grandchildren.

Of course, his father differed. "Hard work will bring you success, son," he would always say. Troy knew it was true, so he worked hard.

He had a dream. He wanted to be the leading neurosurgeon in the region, and he was definitely on the fast track there. Already, hospitals on other islands were contacting him for consultancies and to perform surgeries. His father was proud of him and that was enough to keep him going. He owed so much to his father. Not only had he inspired Troy to become a doctor, he encouraged him to be the best.

Sometimes in the still of the night he knew something was missing from his life. But he pushed it from his mind. No need to get sappy and emotional. A real man focused on what was important, and for now, women were not important.

He loved sex. Loved the feeling of power that came with taking a woman to heaven and joining her there. Loved the sense of vulnerability that came when he lost control for a few moments.

Sandra Walters rushed to his mind. He'd been attracted to her since the first time he'd met her. She'd elicited softer feelings, but he'd pushed those aside. He'd wanted to get her in bed and he did.

The experience was one he wouldn't be forgetting anytime soon. He felt his penis harden. Just thinking about her made him lose control, and he wondered if he'd done the right thing by making love to her. Already he ached for her again, but he anticipated that the moment would pass and things would go back to normal.

He'd seen the look of disgust in her eyes. For a moment he'd felt vulnerable and helpless. He had waited for her to come out of the shower but then he'd seen the look on her face and known what she was about to say. She'd decided she'd made a mistake.

And maybe he had, too. He was accustomed to the occasional woman friend who just wanted to have some fun, cuddle a bit and then return to the warmth of her own bed. No strings attached. A situation that suited him just fine.

So yes, maybe Sandra's attitude had made him face up to reality. Stepping back into his reality was what he needed to do.

Soon enough, Sandra Walters would be back in the U.S. where she belonged.

What startled him was the wave of sadness that washed over him at the thought.

# Chapter 1

*Ten years later*

Sandra could hear the phone ringing. Why did it always happen like this? she wondered, trying to juggle the bag of groceries she carried, her handbag and getting the door opened.

Fortunately, things were on her side. The door clicked open. She pushed it, entered, closed it and raced into the house, dumped the bags on the table and grabbed the phone, realizing that it was Carla calling.

"Sandra, it's Carla. I'm so glad I caught you. I know that it's Saturday and you usually go to the supermarket after work."

"Hi, honey. In fact, I *just* got in from grocery shopping. It's so good to hear you. I wondered when you were going to give me a call. It's long overdue." She kicked her shoes off, walked across the room and lowered herself into the softness of the sofa. Immediately, her weary body started to relax.

"I know," Carla replied. "Unfortunately, I'm not calling to chitchat. I'm calling to ask a favor."

"A favor?" she replied.

"Yes, Shayne and I are going on a Mediterranean cruise in two weeks and we'd like you to take care of the kids for us."

"Me? Are you crazy, Carla? I have no idea how to take care of kids." She rose from the sofa and walked over to the window. *She hadn't heard Carla correctly, had she?*

"Of course I'm not crazy. You're good with the kids. When you were here last summer, they couldn't stop talking about Auntie Sandra. They've already given their seal of approval and are excited about their godmother coming to spend time with them."

"They already think I'm coming? That's not fair," she exclaimed, her gaze focused out the window where a ruby-throated hummingbird sipped from a flower. "You haven't given me a choice. But what about Tamara?"

"I did ask her initially, but I really can't ask her to take care of my two and her two. Four kids under ten years are a bit too much for one person to handle. One of her kids came down with chicken pox. None of mine has had it, so the likelihood of that happening is definitely there."

"You know it's pretty busy around here right now?"

"Sandra, I wonder why you're trying to find excuses," Carla said, a hint of reprimand in her voice. "You know that you can just drop everything and the travel agency will be taken care of. You have a good manager and staff. I know you don't need to be there. Isn't that what you tell me? And there is no need to be scared of the kids. They are generally good."

"Generally? That sounds promising."

"Oh, come on. It's almost a year since you've been here."

Sandra hesitated. She knew exactly what Carla was thinking.

"Worried about Troy?" Carla's words confirmed her suspicion. "I thought you'd agreed to stay away from each other. I don't think you've seen each other more than once a year. Last year, he wasn't even here when you visited."

She hesitated for a moment, watching as the hummingbird flew away. She smiled, knowing that tomorrow it would be back.

"Of course I'm not worried about running into Troy," she finally said, hoping that her voice did not reveal her true feelings. "We see each other when I'm there, but besides polite conversation, I try to keep away from him. In fact, he's the furthest thing from my mind," she said, a bit too emphatically.

Sandra knew she was not telling the whole truth. The sexual tension between the two of them was still there, but she'd forced herself to stay away from him. "Shayne is fine with this arrangement?" she asked, shifting the conversation away from *him*.

She moved from the window, headed back to the sofa and sat. She hated when people made her think about *him*. Tonight, she knew she'd find it difficult to sleep.

"Definitely. In fact, he was the one who suggested I ask you. I think it would be a great opportunity for all involved. Of course, they've already told us we have to call them every day. It's the first time we're not taking them with us, but it's our anniversary and Russell and Tamara have had this all planned for months."

"That's so nice of them. How are Russell and his new wife doing?" Sandra asked.

"They're doing fine. It's almost a year already. No kids on the way yet. Both of them are too busy working, Tori with her singing and Russell globetrotting for CNN. But they both love what they're doing."

"Yes, I noticed Tori's new song debuted at number one on most of the charts. And the video is awesome. I love the fact that she filmed it on the island."

"Yes, she's doing well. Says they are both planning to visit in a few months."

"That must be great. I haven't seen them since they came to Atlanta a few months ago, but Tori always calls."

"Yeah, she likes you."

"I know. I like her, too. She's good for Russell. I'm glad he and Shayne have finally resolved their conflict."

"Yes, me, too. The Knight men are a stubborn bunch."

"Does that mean Darius, too?" Sandra asked.

Carla laughed. "Yes, he is. At ten years old, he has a mind of his own. Sometimes, he seems a bit too mature for his age, and at other times, he's the typical little boy."

"I remember well. I haven't forgotten that trick he played on me last year," Sandra replied, laughing at the memory. "So when do you want me to arrive?" Sandra asked.

"We leave on the thirtieth of June and will be back on the ninth of July. Ten glorious days of sightseeing without a care in the world."

"Sightseeing. I'm sure that's not all you and Shayne are planning," Sandra said slyly.

"I assure you it's not." Carla giggled.

"Just no more kids if you are going to want me to do this babysitting thing again."

"I promise, no more. But look at it like this. This is good practice for when you get your own."

"Me, kids?" Sandra protested. "I'm not sure if that's going to happen anytime soon. I'm wary of men."

"I still believe that you and Troy would make a wonderful couple."

"And here I was thinking you would stop with this matchmaking. Troy? You know how I feel about doctors. They are all alike."

"Sandra, you're being irrational. Just because your father did what he did, doesn't mean all doctors are like that," Carla reasoned.

"I was engaged to one, remember?" she reasoned, unable to keep the bitterness from her voice. "Plus, I've heard enough stories to last me a lifetime. I'll trust a doctor with my physical body and my illnesses, but when it comes to matters of the heart, it's a big *no*. I have no intention of dealing with what my mother did. My father broke her heart and she never recovered."

"You've heard anything about him?" Carla asked.

"My father? The last thing I heard, he was still working at the same hospital, but that's about all I've heard. I just hope he's cheating on the bimbo who married him. Once a cheater, always a cheater."

Carla laughed. "It'd be poetic irony if you end up married to a doctor one day. Don't be surprised if it happens."

"Yes, Carla, my dear," Sandra said, her tone dripping with sarcasm, "Troy and I will have four beautiful kids and live happily ever after."

And as she said it, an image of Troy lying on top of her, his body joined with hers, flashed into her mind.

Carla's laughter halted the erotic slideshow.

When she disconnected the call several minutes later, she did not move.

What had she gotten herself into?

Hopefully, her days in Barbados would pass quickly and she'd return to Atlanta without having to deal with the man who even now continued to haunt her dreams.

Dr. Troy Whitehall stepped out of the meeting room and glanced down at the "missed call" that had registered on his cell phone.

It was Shayne. Something must be wrong. Shayne never called him during his work hours unless it was an emergency.

He quickly hurried to his office at the hospital and pressed Reply on his cell phone.

Shayne answered the phone immediately.

"Troy?"

"What's up, bro?"

"I'm sorry to disturb you at work, but I have a favor to ask. You know that cruise I told you about?" Shayne asked.

"Yes." Troy replied.

"Well, Tamara can't take care of the kids anymore."

"Shayne, you know I don't have that kind of time."

"No, Troy. Carla and I have asked Sandra to come take care of the kids while we're on the cruise. Carla just said that Sandra has agreed. However, I want you to keep an eye on them for me while we're not here."

"Me?" Troy asked. He couldn't believe that Shayne had made such a request.

"I know how you and Sandra feel about each other, but I wouldn't have asked you to do this if it wasn't important. Though the plantation is pretty secure, now that the harvest is over, it will be fairly quiet. With Gladys gone to spend some time with her sister in New York, it'll be only Sandra and the kids in the main house. I want Sandra to know that you'll be there to help her when she needs you. Put your differences aside and think about the kids."

"Okay, man. I'll do it," he said without hesitation. "They are my godchildren, so that does make them my responsibility. I'll still be at the hospital, but I'll make sure I check in each night. I'll try not to annoy the lady."

"I still can't understand what's happened with the two of you. I would have thought you would be perfect for each other. I remember seeing the two of you at my wedding and thinking how comfortable and relaxed you seemed with each other. And of course, I could feel the sizzle."

Troy wondered if this would be a good time to tell Shayne what had happened that night, but he backed out again. He'd planned on several occasions to tell him, but pride had stopped him. He didn't usually fail with the ladies.

"You're still trying to get me hooked up? I'm focused on my career. That fellowship I did in the U.S. last year has me on the fast track to being one of the best neurosurgeons in the Caribbean. I have no immediate plans to give that up. Not even for love."

"Hard words that you may come to regret someday. Never say never."

"I have no problem with spending the rest of my life by myself. I'm content with what I have. I'm happy with my own company—and I have you and George."

"But are you happy? Really happy?"

Troy hesitated. "Yes, I am," he said.

They continued to talk for a while, but when the call finally ended, Troy sat in his office quietly.

He'd lied. He knew he wasn't happy.

But that was life. One didn't have to be happy to have a fulfilled life.

Shayne smiled at his wife as she stepped from the bathroom, a towel wrapped around her.

"I hope we didn't make a serious mistake which will only make matters worse," he said. "Getting both of them to take care of the children while we are away makes sense, doesn't it? They are the obvious choices. With Gladys in New York and Tamara indisposed, we didn't have an alternative."

"That's true, but I know you were thinking that getting the two of them together is a great idea," Carla commented.

"Well, it did cross my mind. I still believe they belong together and whatever is keeping them apart needs to be resolved. Getting them together is the first step. I know both of them will place the kids before their feelings for each other. We have nothing to be worried about."

"I just hope our little plan doesn't backfire."

"Backfire? Don't you see the heat between the two of them whenever they are near each other? That's why I'm glad we have these family functions at least once a year. Forces them to deal with each other. I look at the two of them and it's like they want to eat each other up."

Carla sat on the bed. "I see it, too. It reminds me of you and me."

"Definitely not the situation. But the heat. Yes."

"Also, not the most romantic of situations."

"Yes, but I can remember making love to you many times over that weekend. You left me quite fatigued. It took me weeks to recover."

"I remember I was so angry when I woke up and found you gone."

"But you came back. Four months later. Pregnant."

"Yes, with Darius. When I look at him now, I can't believe that he was born premature. I have to look at the photos of him during that time to remind me of the beautiful miracle God gave us."

"Yes, he's our miracle."

"And a handful, but I'm sure Sandra and Troy can handle him. We do spoil them a bit at times."

"We do. I'm sure Darius will show them his sad, brown eyes and they'll let him do whatever he wants."

"Just like we do," Carla stated.

"Like you do. I always put my foot down."

"Sure you do. I thought we'd decided he won't be getting that Wii."

"He did get an A in the math test at the end of term. And I did promise him anything he wanted."

"Shayne, you know when it comes to your son, you're like a lamb."

"And you are *so* strict and firm."

They both smiled.

"This has been good for us. We've done well."

"Yes, and still love each other, too."

"Want to show me how much you love me, Mr. Knight?" she purred.

"Definitely, I've been wondering how long you're going to keep talking when I'm feeling as horny as a teenager."

And he set out to show her just how much he loved her.

## Chapter 2

Almost two weeks later, Sandra sat on American Airlines Flight 236 wondering if she'd done the right thing. For the past few days, Troy's image had worked its way into her consciousness with greater frequency. She hoped that with Shayne and Carla away, she wouldn't have to see him too often. She suspected he'd drop by to see the kids. He loved them. Hopefully, it wouldn't be too often.

Since the wedding and that passion-filled night, they'd avoided each other. Of course, the occasional meeting had been inevitable, but they'd both dealt with it with maturity. His almost sarcastic politeness had irked her, but she'd returned each of his witty comments with one of her own.

A voice announcing that the flight would soon be

landing drew her from her musings and she sighed in relief. Thirty minutes from Barbados and she was already obsessed with Troy. A wave of dread washed over her and she sighed once again. She sensed the impending doom. They were destined to meet this time.

As the plane descended, she closed her eyes. She was glad the flight had finally come to an end. Though she enjoyed traveling, she didn't like the long hours of inactivity. The four-hour flight to Barbados had been a trying one, especially with the woman and three children who sat behind her. She ached to get up and smack the mother who seemed to have no control over the little terrors. Thank God her godchildren were nothing like that.

She was looking forward to her time on the island. She'd be spending a complete month there. Ten days while Carla and Shayne were away, and a few weeks after they returned.

She'd not had a proper holiday in ages. A week here and a week there, and before she was truly rested, she'd be back at work. Ironically, she didn't have to work as hard as she did. She could, like she was doing now, take some time off when she wanted. She had good, dedicated workers in place, but she was not one to shirk her responsibilities.

She and Carla had started the travel agency, Travelers' Delight, years ago, and only when Carla had married Shayne and decided to settle in Barbados had she agreed to buy Carla's half of the agency.

The flight finally landed. In no time, she'd cleared Immigration and Customs. She loved to travel light, and having only a carry-on eliminated having to wait for luggage.

She'd go into Bridgetown or one of the out-of-town malls to purchase some summer wear if she needed to.

As soon as she exited the building and stepped into the warm sunshine, she knew she'd done the right thing. There was nothing like the combination of sunshine and a cool tropical breeze.

"Sandra, over here."

She turned, recognizing the voice immediately.

Troy.

She'd expected to see him, but not this soon. She felt like turning around and getting back on the plane.

She almost laughed at her own illogical thought, but she breathed deeply, plastered a hopefully cheerful smile on her face and walked in his direction.

"Troy," she said when she finally reached him. She could hear her heart racing.

"Sandra," he replied, nodding politely. He reached for her bag, taking it from her. Immediately, he turned and headed for the parking lot.

She followed reluctantly, the joy of being there already slowly dissipating.

But she couldn't help but notice that he looked good. He'd changed his style since she'd last seen him. He now wore a close-cropped haircut complemented by a neatly trimmed mustache, beard and sideburns.

He'd been less conservative with short dreads, so the change was an interesting one. It suited him, made him look more mature and…sexier.

When they reached the car, he placed the suitcase in the trunk and then opened the passenger side for her.

*At least he still knows how to be a gentleman.*

She stepped cautiously, trying her hardest not to touch him.

Several minutes later, they were driving along the ABC Highway, which she knew stretched all the way to the north of the island.

The tension in the car crackled, and Sandra was amazed that after all these years her attraction to him still unsettled her stomach.

For a while she sat in silence, concentrating on the several changes that had taken place since her last visit.

She continued to be amazed at the changing landscape along the highway. New residential developments seem to pop up like weeds each time she visited. It was sad in a way, since with each new development more of the island's rich foliage disappeared. One of the things she loved about the island was that past efforts had been made to preserve the island's natural beauty.

"How was the flight?" he finally asked politely.

"It was fine," she replied briefly. She didn't want to encourage conversation.

"From the expression on your face, I can tell it really wasn't fine."

"I'm not too thrilled about flying, but it's an inevitable part of my work," she replied. "I just find the inactivity unappealing, and of course, a woman with three spoiled kids didn't make the hours go any faster. But I'm glad to be here." There goes my attempt to be brief, she thought.

"That's good," he responded.

For a while there was silence, the only sound the occasional hum of a passing car.

"I am hoping that my being around won't upset you too much," he finally said. His voice was calm, his tone neutral.

"Your being around?" she replied, trying to appear indifferent.

"Well, Shayne did ask me to keep an eye on you and the kids."

"He did?" She tried to control her dismay.

"Yes, didn't Carla tell you?" There was genuine surprise in his voice.

"She didn't."

"Well, you are here and I'm sure that we can behave like two mature adults. It's only for ten days," he said nonchalantly.

"It really doesn't bother me, Troy. Too many years have passed for me to dwell on our one night. That's water under the bridge." Her body trembled, belying her assertion.

"Good, I'm glad you feel that way. I take my responsibilities seriously, and since Shayne asked, I intend to make sure that all of you are just fine."

"I'm sure we'll be all right," she said forcefully.

"Good, don't want the kids to feel that all is not well with us. We're going to have to shake on that. New beginning."

For the rest of the ride they remained silent, both

immersed in their thoughts; both still aware of each other.

When the car pulled into the driveway of the Knight Plantation, both felt a sense of relief. These ten days were going to be a lot more difficult to handle, more than they could've imagined.

As soon as the door closed behind Troy, Sandra turned to Carla.

"So, Troy and I are supposed to be assisting each other with the kids. Now why do I find it strange that you didn't mention that to me during our conversation?"

"I didn't?" Carla replied, trying to feign surprise. "I was sure I mentioned it when I told you about the cruise. Didn't I tell you that Troy would be dropping by?"

"Yes, you did tell me dropping by, but you didn't mention that he'll be doing it every night."

"Oh, dear. I didn't realize that's what he thought. I'm going to have a serious talk with Shayne. He knows how the two of you feel about each other. Of course, I can never understand why you feel the way you do about Troy. One of these days, you're going to have to tell me the truth."

"There is nothing going on between Troy and me. Yes, we did have a sort of misunderstanding, but that's been taken care of. We both agreed tonight that for the sake of the kids, we'll try to be cordial to each other."

"That's a good start. I knew both of you would see reason. While the plantation is relatively secure at night with the watchman on duty, I'll still feel better if Troy came over occasionally to make sure that everything is all right. He's a doctor. If anything happens, he'll know what to do."

"I said it's not a problem. Troy means nothing to me. He's just a friend of yours and Shayne's. There is nothing that says that we have to be bosom buddies."

"That is very true," Carla replied. She glanced up at the clock on the wall.

"It's almost midnight. I have to get some sleep. Our flight leaves around midday."

"I'm feeling a bit tired, too. Have a good night."

"You, too, honey. Sweet dreams," she added.

Sweet dreams?

Sandra had no doubt that her dreams would be filled with the image of the sexy Troy Whitehall!

The next morning was a hive of activity. Like busy bees, everyone helped the anniversary couple to pack and get out of the house. Amidst kisses and hugs and a few tears, Shayne and Carla waved goodbye and were soon on their way to the Grantley Adams International Airport.

Minutes later, their parents forgotten, Sandra's two godchildren stood looking up at her.

"So what are we going to do, godmother?" asked Darius, his eyes wide with excitement. "I'm hungry. Can I have some ice cream?"

Sandra smiled. "Well, Darius, I could give you some ice cream, but that means you won't get any tonight with dinner."

"But Mommy gives me ice cream every day," he stated, his eyes all wide and innocent.

"Oh, she told me. You're allowed some ice cream in the evening after dinner. It's now ten o'clock in the morning."

"She told you?" he asked.

"Yes, she did. I've been made aware of all your tricks."

Lynn-Marie giggled. "I want to go play with my dolls. You want to have a tea party?"

"Yuck," Darius responded, his face distorted with disgust. "I'm going to go play with my Wii. I have this awesome new game."

"I'm going to go play with your sister for a while and then I'll come and play with you, Darius."

"You can play video games? You're old."

Sandra couldn't help but laugh. "Yes, I can play video games and I'm not that old. I'm younger than your dad."

"And you're pretty like my mom."

"Oh, thank you," she said. "And you're handsome, too."

"Oh, I know. I hear Mom's friends say it all the time. 'He's as handsome as his dad.'"

"Well, I can see you're going to be a heartbreaker."

"Thank you, Auntie Sandra. I'm going to go play for a while. You can come to the playroom when you're ready."

"I'll make sure I do," she replied. With that, he turned and raced out the door.

Lynn-Marie just stared at her brother and then turned to Sandra. "I'm still hungry."

"Come, I'll fix something for you."

"Can I have a hot dog?"

"Sure, I'll do one for you and then we'll go play house."

"We can have a tea party?"

"Sound good. We'll have hot dogs and I'll make some sandwiches for the dolls."

"Thanks, Auntie Sandra. Daisy," she said, lifting the doll in her hands, "loves cheese sandwiches."

Sandra smiled. Her godchildren were really special. Maybe they'd help to keep *his* image from her mind.

A gentle breeze blew from the east, caressing her face as she pushed Lynn-Marie on the swing. Exhausted by the summer heat and the excitement of their parents' departure, the kids had fallen asleep after lunch and had slept for most of the afternoon. Darius, a remote in his hand, seemed content to let his car race around the garden. On the swing, Lynn-Marie squealed in delight as she went higher and higher.

The sound of an engine caused her to turn in the direction of the silver SUV coming up the driveway.

Immediately, her heart rate increased. It was Troy.

The vehicle stopped in the parking area and he slowly climbed out.

She could tell at once he was tired. He must have had a hard day at work.

"Hi, kids," he said, the smiled he reserved for the kids on his face.

Darius and Lynn-Marie had already raced over to him, hugging him around the legs.

"Guess what I brought for you," he said.

"What, Uncle Troy?" they both said.

"I'm hoping your Auntie Sandra doesn't mind, but I know how much you like pizza."

"Oh, good," Darius squealed. "I hope it has pineapple on it."

"Pineapple, pineapple," Lynn-Marie said, jumping up and down. "I love pineapple."

"There are two pizzas, with all the toppings you like and of course, extra cheese." He turned to face Sandra. "Let's just hope your house guest likes pizza, too," he said.

"I like pizza fine," she replied abruptly. She was annoyed. He should have called and told her he was bringing pizza. Her plans to grill burgers had been ruined.

"Good, I'll get them from the car."

"No, you stay with the kids. I'll get them and take care of everything. I'll make a salad to go with the pizza."

"Okay, I'll stay and play with the kids. I think I can still remember how to entertain them," he said turning to them.

Sandra walked over to the car, taking the two large boxes out, and headed for the house.

When she entered the house and closed the door, she stopped, placed her back against the door and breathed in deeply. She had to get herself under control. She couldn't allow herself to be like this each time he was near. If she did, the next ten days were going to be unbearable.

She thought she'd learned to deal with her feelings for him, but it seemed that whenever he was near they would awaken from their dormant state.

She breathed deeply again and, feeling more in control, walked briskly to the kitchen. She loved cooking and was looking forward to doing so for the kids. She was still annoyed that her dinner plans had been ruined, but she couldn't allow Troy to continue to rattle her composure. She'd do the salad and put on a smile, and he'd never know how she felt.

She made one of her favorite salads—fresh lettuce and cucumbers, with sweet peppers, raisins and sweetened cranberries. She tossed everything in a large salad bowl and sprinkled grated cheese on the top.

Of course, she checked the freezer for ice cream and realized that Carla had stocked it with enough to last for some time. She'd just have to make sure Darius didn't get his hands on it when he wasn't supposed to.

She heard the sound of feet running down the hallway. The kids raced into the room and came to a halt on reaching her. Troy strolled in behind them.

"We're hungry for pizza."

"Okay, go wash your hands and come back. Darius, you help Lynn-Marie."

"I will, Auntie Sandra," he replied. "Come, Lynn-Marie." He took her hand and led her outside.

The atmosphere changed, becoming charged with enough electricity to light all the bulbs in the room.

"I should have called and asked you about dinner,"

Troy said apologetically. "I know Carla is very particular about the kids eating healthy, but I know she does allow them the occasional pizza."

"Oh, the pizzas are fine," she said, a smile plastered on her face. "I did plan on grilling burgers, but tomorrow is another day. Please don't feel that you need to bring dinner each time you come here. If you let me know in advance, I'll make sure I include you in our meals."

"I'm sorry. It didn't cross my mind that you'd be cooking. You're on holiday, and I don't want you to be cooking every day. I'm sure taking care of kids must be something you're not accustomed to."

"That may be true, but I've spent enough time here over the past few years that I have an idea what they like and don't like. I can handle them."

"Sorry, I didn't mean to insult you. Just making an observation."

"So can I expect you to drop by every night?" she asked.

Before he could respond, Darius, still holding his sister's hand, reappeared.

"We're done."

"Good. I've finished setting the table. We're ready to eat."

Darius raced to his seat and then realized he'd forgotten his sister.

"Come, Lynn-Marie. Sit next to me."

Lynn-Marie smiled adoringly at her brother and raced to stand next to him. He lifted her into a chair.

Dinner was a riot of easy chatter about the kids'

day, and Troy's day, which lost the kids' attention. The TV channel was changed to Animal Planet at Darius's insistence.

Sandra avoided looking directly at Troy. At moments, she could feel his eyes on her, staring, probing, but she kept her eyes on the television and the kids.

When the kids were done, Darius asked, "Can I go take my shower now? I'll read until I get sleepy. Uncle Troy, can you come tuck me in?"

"Sure, buddy. I'll come up in a bit. You want a story, too?"

"No, it's fine. I read to myself before I go to bed. Auntie Sandra has to read to Lynn-Marie."

Sandra took the opportunity to speak. "Come, Lynn-Marie, let's go give you your bath and then it's time for bed."

"And a story?"

"Yes, I heard your brother."

"I have a *Princess and the Frog* book. I want to hear that story again."

When Sandra left Lynn-Marie's room a half hour later, slightly damp and covered in the scent of powder, she could not help but smile.

When she stepped into the kitchen, it was to find Troy at the sink washing the dishes.

She stopped, surprised by what he was doing. She'd never seen him as the domestic kind.

When he wiped his hand and turned around, she could not help but laugh out loud. He wore a frilly apron around his waist.

He looked down sheepishly at the apron. "I couldn't find anything else. Didn't want to ruin my trousers."

"It's fine. Just strange to see you like this."

Troy unwrapped the apron from around him and placed it on the rung.

"Thanks, you didn't have to," she said.

"It's okay. I don't have a problem with washing up. Darius fell asleep before he could open the book," he replied.

"I'm not surprised. He'd been going all day. He did sleep a bit during the afternoon, but I was beginning to think he'd never get tired."

"Yes, he does have lots of energy."

For a while they were silent. "How was your first day with the kids?" Troy finally asked.

"It was fine. It's a lot easier that I thought. The kids are really good. They occupy themselves most of the time. Lynn-Marie only needs her dolls to make her happy, and Darius his Wii and computer. I'm always amazed at how mature Darius is for his age. I keep forgetting he's ten. And Lynn-Marie, she's a teenager trapped in a four-year-old's body. I just have to keep them fed and they're happy."

"That's good, though not much of a holiday for you."

"Oh, it's really good. I'm getting some rest. The past few months have been really busy at work. I love Darius and Lynn-Marie. This is a chance to spend some time with them."

"I'll help as much as I can. We can take them out… to the movie, the beach…."

"I don't want to impose on your time. I know how busy you are with that career of yours," she commented.

"No problem. We can do stuff on my days off. I work four days and then have the next two off. It's a good schedule."

"And you *take* those off days?" Sandra asked.

"Not all the time, but I can take them now. The kids are important."

He paused for a moment, as if he was trying to find the words to say. "It's good to see you, Sandra. You look good."

"Thanks. So do you. But I'd prefer if we don't go there."

"Why? Because you know I'm still attracted to you? That I still want you, even after all these years?" he said.

"And you ignore me whenever I'm here. You didn't say two words to me when I came to Russell and Tori's wedding," she chided.

"But that's what you wanted. Ever since we made love ten years ago, you've treated me like scum. I thought we were adults. You didn't want any commitment, neither did I."

"That was then, but maybe *I* want more now. You'll never give me that. You want your career and some convenient sex. And that's fine for you."

He stopped. What she was saying was true. He wanted her, but he didn't want commitment. But the way she said it made it sound so…repugnant.

"I'm sorry. I didn't know that's how you felt."

"I didn't expect anything more. You're a doctor," she said snidely.

"And my being a doctor means that I'm like that. You're not being rational. Just because you've had a bad experience with a doctor doesn't mean we're all bad."

"You're all good at medicine but you're not good at relationships. I see it all the time. Too busy working, too many dreams, and then the sexy nurses."

He didn't respond.

"But I don't want to talk about this," she continued. "I'm going up and take a shower and then take out a book and read until I'm sleepy. Thanks for the pizza."

"I think it's about time I left. Make sure you lock the door behind me."

He turned abruptly and left the room. She followed him and slowed when she caught up with him at the door.

He turned and she could see the anger in his eyes.

"I'll see you tomorrow," he said abruptly. Desire flamed in his eyes.

He reached for her, his lips finding hers in a bruising kiss. At first she resisted, and then the warmth coursed through her body and she remembered how sweet he tasted and the appealing scent of aftershave that still lingered after a day's work.

As abruptly as the kiss started, it ended.

"And you say you don't want me?"

He eased the door open and stepped outside, closing it behind him.

Sandra stood there quietly, her body betraying her control.

Yes, she wanted him.

Troy struggled with his fatigue. He wasn't even sure if the lethargy was a result of his interaction with Sandra or work, or a combination of both. He didn't like how she made him feel.

Tonight, he was sure sleep would not come to him easily. He glanced at his watch. It was just after nine o'clock. When he reached the roundabout at Hothersal Turning, he took the left turn. He needed someone to talk to, and George was the only one available.

He didn't know what George could tell him about his feelings for Sandra, but he just wanted to talk to someone who would understand. He loved George and Shayne like brothers, in high school they'd been inseparable. The Knight plantation had always been a second home for him and George.

They had all been at the university when tragedy had struck and forever changed Shayne's life. They had returned home with Shayne. He remembered it as if it were yesterday. It had been just after exams and they'd gone to Trinidad to celebrate. The celebration had come to an abrupt end. When Shayne's parents had died, they had all been devastated.

He'd never seen Shayne cry before, but that day, his strong, confident best friend had held on to him and cried his heart out.

The next day, Shayne had transformed into a mature

individual who was now responsible for the welfare of his younger brother and sister.

He'd dealt with the funeral arrangements without the slightest sign of reluctance, and the day of the funeral he'd become a man, denying his own need to grieve while he remained strong for the twins, Russell and Tamara.

Shayne's friends had helped him to take care of the twins and the plantation.

He'd even been there when Darius was born, a tiny preemie, small enough to fit in the palm of Shayne's hand. He'd seen a Shayne he'd never seen before. Without hesitation Shayne had taken responsibility for the twins. He'd watched how Shayne had transformed into a man with responsibilities. Shayne had put his teenage years of partying behind and become a man. The Shayne that existed now was a confident, focused individual who'd taken control of his life.

Troy frowned. Even though he was successful, he often felt that he'd lost control of who he was.

One thing he did know was that Shayne had found love, that wonderful, true love that meant forever. He saw it each time Shayne looked at Carla. At times, he felt an envy so strong, he wasn't sure if the feeling was real.

He cleared his mind of the past and pulled into the driveway of the house where George lived, a massive structure nestled among the canopies of numerous royal palms.

If he didn't have any intentions of getting married, then George would definitely not be on the market.

George loved sex and women, but that was only the George which others saw. Troy knew him better than anyone else.

He'd been there when George's former girlfriend, Rachel Davis, had married a man almost twice her age and left the island. True, George had ended the relationship, but the marriage had taken place four months after the breakup. George had seemed to be taking it all in stride, but Troy had known differently. He'd been the one to offer comfort to his ever-so-in-control friend when he'd broken down and cried. That was the second time he'd seen George cry, and it had convinced him that love was more pain than pleasure.

He drove up to the house, knowing that George would be alone. George had a policy that he stuck firmly to: love 'em and leave 'em. In other words, you do the loving at their home then leave and head back to yours. George never brought women to his house. Troy smiled. He was convinced that one day George was going to fall again, and fall hard.

He parked his car quickly next to George's BMW and hopped out. Before he could reach the door, it opened and George stood there, looking as fit as he always did.

"Hi, bro, what's up?" He heard concern in George's voice.

"Just wanted to drop by. Is it a problem?" he asked.

"Come off it, Troy. What nonsense are you asking?" George asked. "When has your dropping by ever been a problem? You're getting a bit too sensitive in your old age."

"Sorry, man. I don't know what came over me."

"Yeah, you're acting like Shayne used to before he got married."

"Man, how could you say that about your best friend? Especially when he's not here to defend himself."

"Man, come inside. I'm about to eat. You hungry?"

"No, just came from eating."

"Eating? You had a date?" he asked, and then he paused, his eyes widening with awareness. "Oh, now I see. Shayne and Carla left yesterday, didn't they?" A knowing smile lit his face up. "Now I know what's wrong. It's Sandra Walters that has your boxers all tied up in knots."

"If you're going to make fun of me, I'm going to go."

"Got that underused penis of yours all hard and ready. It's about time. You haven't had a good lay in months." George chuckled.

"Sandra's not that kind of girl. She won't just jump into bed with me." She *had* jumped into bed with him, but he had to defend her.

"Oh, I know she's not that kind of girl, but I do know she had the hots for you."

"Man, I'm over her. She means nothing to me."

George laughed out loud and it echoed like thunder through the room.

"So what are you doing here? Usually you're so caught up in your work, Shayne and I don't hear from you too often."

He heard the sarcasm in George's voice and he knew he deserved everything his friend was saying. It was true. He'd become so caught up with his job, he rarely had time for his friends. He hadn't even seen his godchildren in months, until Shayne had called.

There was no need to respond. He lowered his head in shame.

When he did look up, George had a strange look on his face.

"You're going to have to decide one day what you want. As you said, Sandra's not that kind of girl. You want a romp or you want more? I'm sure she's attracted to you enough that if you pushed the issue she'd give in. But what more do you want to offer her?"

"You're the last person that should be talking. You're unmerciful when it comes to women."

"I assure you I'm not. None of the women I deal with have any expectations. They're single women who are comfortable in their independence and don't want to get married. The day I meet a woman like Sandra who wants me, I'll be putting on my suit and tie and standing at the top of the aisle waiting for her."

"But you know I have no intentions of getting married anytime soon. Maybe when I'm fifty. Right now, I want to focus on my career."

"Your career! That's all we hear about. Even now, you're still trying to live for your father. Do you need his approval so much that you live for him and not yourself?"

Troy did not respond at first. George's words were so close to the truth that there was no sense in denying them.

"Since you don't have a father, you won't know what it's like." Before the words left his lips, he regretted them—more so when he saw the look of utter pain on his friend's face.

"I didn't mean that, George. Sorry, that was wrong." He moved closer to his friend, giving him one of those big, bear hugs they would use in times of sadness.

"It's okay." George grinned. "I deserve it. I didn't mean to knock you so hard," he responded, returning the hug with the full force of his bulging biceps and triceps.

"Especially when you're in the same situation I'm in. I don't see you making any attempt to commit to someone," Troy said.

"Okay. Okay," George replied, pushing him away.

"I hear you, but back to what we've been talking about," Troy commented. "I've been thinking about my relationship with Sandra. Maybe it's time the both of us start thinking about our future. You see how happy Shayne and Carla are? Tamara and Kyle? Russell and Tori? Don't you ever think of what they have? What we don't have?"

"Yeah. All the time." George had gone suddenly silent and pensive, his expression troubled.

"I was totally content until my friends started getting married."

"I know exactly what you mean," George said sadly.

For a while they sat in silence.

Troy realized in that moment that he loved George in a way that was hard to explain. They were not brothers by blood, but the feelings that existed between them came from a foundation cemented by loyalty and strong devotion.

Tonight made him realize that he wanted to experience what Shayne had.

But more so, he wished happiness for his friend. If anyone needed a woman who would love him unconditionally, it was George.

He just hoped they wouldn't end up as they were now—two very lonely men.

# Chapter 3

Sandra woke on Saturday morning irritated by a lack of sleep. It had taken her hours before she had finally drifted into a restless sleep filled with vivid images of a naked Troy.

She was beginning to think that she'd made the biggest mistake in coming to the island. But immediately she realized that being with her godchildren was worth the inconvenience of having *him* around.

Next to her, Lynn-Marie lay fast asleep. She'd not heard the little girl when she came in. She rose slowly from the bed, careful not to wake the sleeping child.

Six o'clock. When she was in Barbados she could rarely sleep late. She rose with the sun, almost as if she needed to see the awakening sun as it cast its first tender rays on the island.

Of course, by midday, those same rays would lose their gentle spirit, sharing their heat with a mean generosity that only the strong Atlantic winds could relieve.

Outside, the plantation was slowly coming alive. In the distance, a lone worker headed out to the fields to perform the few tasks that were still required now that the harvest was over.

She wondered if Darius was up. He, too, woke early, but preferred to remain in bed watching his favorite cartoon on Nickelodeon.

She showered and dressed quickly and headed downstairs.

Today, she was taking the kids on a visit to Harrison's Cave and then stopping at a popular restaurant for an early dinner. Yesterday, they'd remained at home, spending the day watching movies and playing snakes and ladders.

Whenever she came to the island she never failed to visit the cave, the island's most popular tourist attraction. For the past two years, the cave had been under renovations, so she was excited to see what improvements had been made. Even before these changes, the magnificent, crystallized limestone cavern with its pure clear water and flowing streams had always left her in awe of the beauty of nature.

Downstairs, she entered the kitchen and quickly scrambled eggs and made toast. As she took down bowls and an array of cereal, Darius entered, leading his sister.

"Good morning, Auntie Sandra," they said.

"And morning to both of you," she said, giving them each a hug and a kiss on the forehead.

Lynn-Marie laughed. "You kiss just like Mommy."

"Breakfast on the table in five minutes," Sandra said.

"Good," Darius replied. "I'm so hungry."

As Sandra poured milk into two cups and placed them on the table, the phone rang.

She picked it up.

"Hello, Sandra, this is Troy."

"Morning," she replied. Her heart began to thump rapidly.

"What are the plans for today? I'm off, so I'm willing to spend the day with the kids."

"We'll be fine, Troy."

"Sandra, let's not make this difficult. I'm off. I can help out. I want to see the kids." She could hear the annoyance in his voice.

"Okay," she conceded. "I'm taking the kids to Harrison's Cave. Then we'll go out for something to eat."

"Good, I'm coming."

"Are you sure? The kids are a handful."

"Then I will definitely come. You need someone to help you. When do you plan to leave?"

"Around midday."

"Good. I'll be there. I just need to drop something off at the hospital. I'll call Harrison's Cave to make sure I can get a ticket."

"Okay, I'll see you at midday. We'll be ready."

"Bye," he said before he disconnected the call.

She put the phone down and turned to the kids.

"That was your Uncle Troy. He's coming with us today."

"Where are we going?"

"We're going to Harrison's Cave and then Uncle Troy is taking us to get dinner."

Lynn-Marie clapped while her brother cheered. They could not contain their excitement.

"Okay, let's eat quickly," Darius shouted eagerly.

"Take your time. There is no need to hurry. We have the whole morning to do nothing. Uncle Troy is coming around midday."

"Okay, Auntie Sandra," he replied.

For the next half hour, Sandra sat listening to the children talk about everything and nothing in particular. The rest of the morning they spent watching one of Lynn-Marie's favorite movies, until she sent Darius to his room to get ready while she took care of Lynn-Marie.

When Troy arrived just before midday, they were already sitting on the verandah waiting for him. Of course, the kids had kept asking the time until his vehicle pulled into the driveway. Darius immediately jumped up, anxious to get on their way. Sitting quietly was not one of his favorite activities.

Troy stepped out of the car, dressed all comfortable and casual. She'd never really seen him dressed like this. Most of the time, he was either dressed for work or semiformally dressed. Today, he wore jeans and a close-fitting graphic T-shirt that displayed his well-toned body.

As always, his presence made her uneasy. She tried

to keep her eyes on the kids, but they shifted back to watch him as he walked up the steps.

Darius was the first to speak. "Hi, Uncle Troy. I'm ready."

"Hi, Uncle Troy," echoed Lynn-Marie, showing him her colorful picture book. "I'm ready, too."

"That's good. From the look of your Auntie Sandra, I can see she's ready, too. Good, let's go."

She could feel his eyes on her. She finally turned to look at him, noticing a strange expression on his face.

"Thanks for offering to come with us," she said, realizing that she meant it.

"A change of heart?" he asked. When she only smiled he continued, "I was able to book a ticket online, so all is well for me to join you on the tour."

"That's good. The kids are going to love it there," she replied. "It's definitely something to see."

"I haven't been in ages, but I've heard the changes are spectacular," Troy said.

"I'll go get my bag and we'll be ready."

She smiled briefly at him and watched as he moved to sit with the kids. She could tell he loved them. She wondered what kind of father he'd make and immediately concluded that he'd probably be a good one. Until he got caught up with his work or some young nurse got her hooks into him.

She walked up the stairs, shaking her head. She really should give him the benefit of the doubt. He was really good with the kids. Maybe she needed to stop equating every doctor she met with her father or her ex-fiancé. Troy seemed a good man and, despite his work, he was taking his responsibility with the kids seriously.

For the briefest of moments, she allowed her mind to drift back to the night when they'd made love. The chemistry between them had been intense. She would have to admit at that time she'd felt a connection to him that went beyond the incredible sex they'd had.

At times, when she visited the island and came in contact with him, she'd noticed special things about him; things that made her wonder if she'd been too hasty in deciding that a relationship with him was not a good thing. The way his face lit up when he was talking about cricket, the rare laughter that transformed the usual serious expression on his face; those were the times she felt an ache and emptiness so strong that she longed for what she'd rejected.

Perhaps her father's betrayal had wounded her more than she was willing to admit. Troy reminded her too much of her father with his devotion to work. At that time, Troy had been dedicated to his work, and anything else was considered an unnecessary distraction. She understood clearly his dedication to his work, but she never wanted to be second in importance to the man she loved and married.

The day after they'd made love, he'd made it quite clear that she would be a distraction. She'd expected it. For doctors, work came first. Little did he know she'd overheard his conversation with Shayne that evening.

"Oh, she's fine. A sexy little number. But you know me, Shayne. I'm all about my work. Nothing's going to distract me from achieving my dreams."

She had stood outside the kitchen, but at his words she'd tiptoed away, a sharp pain in her chest. She had gone to her room and cried until her hurt had transformed to anger.

She'd vowed that Troy Whitehall would never hurt her again. He wanted to dangle a juicy red apple in front of her, tempt her to eat and then walk away.

Forcing herself from the past, Sandra took her handbag up, glanced in the mirror, nodded in approval and then headed back down the stairs.

When she reached the verandah, the kids already had their shoes on and from their expression, were impatiently waiting on her.

She sighed, a response that was becoming a habit when Troy was around.

She would need all of her strength to fight her renewed feelings for Troy, but she knew now how to deal with his magnetic pull. His words that evening long ago still rang in her head.

The drive to Harrison's Cave, located in the lush, grassy central region of the island, took them about thirty minutes. The trip was not only for the kids; seeing the improvements was important for the travel agency. Barbados was one of the popular destinations in the Caribbean, and her love for the island was obvious whenever she talked about its beauty to prospective clients.

The cave, situated in the parish of St. Thomas, was rediscovered in 1974 and eventually developed by the Government of Barbados. Today, it was one of the island's main attractions. Some Bajans even dared to call it the Eighth Wonder of the World.

Sitting in a tram along with Troy, the kids and several visitors to the island, Sandra breathed in deeply in anticipation of the journey ahead. She'd been glad when the guide had told her that the kids had to sit with an adult. She had feared she would have to sit next to Troy, but with two persons per seat, she held on to Lynn-Marie with a sigh of relief.

The tram moved slowly downward, the guide's voice echoing in the subtly lit passageway down which they traveled. When the tram entered, there was a stirring of voices that rose to sounds of delight and excitement. Breathtakingly beautiful stalagmites and stalactites grew from the floor and roof of the cave. To the left, calm glassy pools beckoned. In the distance, the rush of water could be heard.

When the guide, who'd introduced himself as Tyrone, told them they could disembark, she hopped off the tram with as much excitement as the kids.

She inhaled slowly, as if she expected the spirit of the cave would somehow give her strength.

She glanced across at Troy. His head turned and their eyes met, the expression on his face strange and unexpected. Heat flashed there and he made no attempt to hide it.

She eventually glanced away. She'd not expected his reaction, his blatant desire and need.

"Auntie, isn't it pretty?" Lynn-Marie's tiny hand gripped hers, shaking it with excitement. Her other hand pointed upward to a beautiful stalactite illuminated by floodlights.

"Yes, it is, honey."

"Can I carry home one of the 'stalac' things?"

"I'm sorry, Lynn-Marie. You can't. If you do, it'll mean that no one else can come here and see them."

"Okay," she replied, childish acceptance on her face.

Tyrone ordered them back into the tram and the journey continued. With each cavern, more of the cave's beauty was revealed, so when the tram exited the cave half an hour later, oohs and aahs and applause indicated their satisfaction. The words *fantastic* and *amazing* came immediately to mind. Lynn-Marie continued to comment on how pretty the cave was and how beautiful the 'stalac' things were and she continued to lament that she would have liked to have one of them for her room.

Leaving the cave, they took the drive back to the city, stopping at a local restaurant that Troy claimed had the best grilled chicken and salads.

After the meal was completed and the kids were full and in the nearby playground, Sandra sat quietly, unsure of what to say.

Eventually, Troy broke the silence.

"You've been enjoying spending time with the kids?" he said.

"Absolutely. They are good kids," she responded.

"Shayne and Carla have done a great job. They are great parents."

"One of the things I admire about them, which I don't see with most kids these days, is the fact that they love to read. They have their Nintendo and iPods and computers, but they still love to read."

"Shayne and Carla encouraged it. We were told that for every gift we give the kids, we should also include a book. As a result, they don't only have to read, they enjoy reading," Troy said.

"And do you read, beyond your medical books?" she asked.

"I try to as often as I can. I'm actually reading through the Harry Potter books right now and have reached book five. I wanted to see what the whole hoopla was about. It takes me a few months to finish each one, but I'm actually enjoying them. I'm enjoying them much more than the movies."

"It's true. Movie adaptations rarely surpass the quality of the books. I am a bit surprised. I don't see you as much of a fiction reader," she commented.

"Why am I not surprised to hear that? You still don't think much of me, do you? Do you hate men so much?"

"And why would you say that? I love men fine. Just because I'm not willing to hop into bed at the drop of a hat doesn't mean I'm a man-hater," she responded, slightly miffed.

"I'm sorry. I didn't mean it that way. You have made it quite clear you're not into relationships…or doctors."

"Doctors, definitely."

"So you don't go to one? We do serve a purpose."

"Oh, I'm fine with my annual examination and under professional circumstances."

"So why the dislike for us in relation to relationships?"

"It's the age old adage—once bitten, twice shy. I actually had two relationships with doctors. One of the things I've noticed is that your life isn't your own. You live and breathe medicine, and working in the hospital can be very demanding. I once had a fiancé who was a doctor. I can't count the number of missed dates we had. It's not that I have a problem with doctors. I just don't think they're made for good relationships."

"Isn't your father a doctor?" he asked.

"Yes, the more reason for how I feel," she replied, years of pent-up anger rising to the surface. "I saw my beautiful, vivacious mother become a weak, pale imitation of who she was. My father never spent time with us. He was always busy. But along with that he cheated on her for years until he finally left her and married one of the nurses. When my mother died, they said it was a heart attack, but I knew it was a broken heart. He killed her." She slammed her hand on the table, unable to control the rush of anger and sadness surging through her body. A half-filled paper cup tipped over.

"I'm sorry to hear about that," he responded calmly, reaching for the cup and wiping the table with a napkin. She could hear the sympathy in his voice. "My father is a doctor, and though he worked long hours, I have never questioned his love for my mother. From what I can see, they have a good relationship."

"I'm sure they do," she said sarcastically.

"I'm not saying that it's perfect, but my mother has always been supportive of my father and he supportive of her," he responded.

"She's a housewife, right?"

"Yes, she is, but that doesn't mean she's unhappy. That's a choice she made. My father has always emphasized the importance of following your dreams. In my case, he may be vehement about it, but he's never ever forced me into doing anything I didn't want."

"And your mother is happy? Has she achieved all she wanted in life?" she asked.

"I should think so."

"I'm going to bet that she had to compromise. Gave up all she wanted in life to make your father happy. Somewhere in her past is an unfulfilled dream."

"Maybe, but isn't that what marriage should be about? Compromise?"

"Ironically, it's always the men who say so. And of course, they're usually the ones who don't compromise. It's always the women who give up their dreams. Do you think he would have stayed at home if she was the one who wanted to be a doctor?" she argued.

He didn't say anything, his face etched with concern.

"Maybe you're right. Maybe we don't think much about all this. However, I still believe it's something that must be decided by the two persons involved…the two persons who love each other. Isn't that what love is all about? Selflessness?"

"Maybe, but I'm not sure if I see it that way. I don't want to end up losing a part of myself to make someone else happy."

"I'm not sure my mother gave up a part of herself. I know you see what she did as compromising. I know my father is a tyrant when it comes to achievement, but I've never had any doubt that he loved me and my mother. The reality is that if we weren't willing to work long hours, we wouldn't be able to save lives."

"I understand that. Maybe I'm being selfish, but I don't know if that's what I'd want. I don't know if I want to be there in the background while my husband's devotion centers on his work and his patients."

He stared at her for a while, but before she could respond, Lynn-Marie and Darius dashed out of the playground.

"I'm ready to go home, Uncle Troy. You told us to come when we get tired. Lynn-Marie says she's feeling tired and I want to watch my favorite show. It begins at six o'clock."

"Then your wish is my command," he replied, ruffling Darius's hair. He turned to Sandra. "We're going to have to continue this conversation at a later date."

She nodded, although she wondered what else could be said about the situation. They'd both made their opinions clear.

She followed as Troy and the kids walked out of the restaurant ahead of her. She stared at him as he walked away.

She couldn't help it; there was something sexy and sensual about the way Troy walked.

She suppressed her feelings, but the conversation with him had released some of the tension she felt inside. She'd seen a little bit into his mind and heart, but the barrier she had built to separate them still stood.

While the conversation had made both of their

positions clear, it had done nothing to change her feelings for him. She didn't think she could ever resolve her opinion about doctors. He was one, and that made the emotions he stirred in her even more bewildering.

Even now, sitting in the car, her awareness of him didn't fail to send tingles along her spine. Glancing at the backseat, she realized the kids had fallen asleep, and the silence in the car made her wonder if he could hear the pounding of her heart.

When the car finally pulled into the driveway, she wanted to jump out and race to her room, but she had to help with the kids.

When the car stopped, she stepped out quickly, wanting to get away from him before she was under his spell.

She opened the rear door and picked Lynn-Marie up. The little girl did not stir. Darius, next to her, came slowly awake.

"Are we home?' he asked, rubbing his eyes and stretching.

"Yes," she replied. "I'll take your sister up to her room and Uncle Troy will make sure you take a bath before you start watching TV."

They followed Sandra into the house.

When Sandra came back downstairs, Troy was nowhere to be seen. He'd stayed upstairs with Darius longer than she'd expected.

In the kitchen, she placed water in a kettle to boil, and searched to make sure her favorite Earl Gray tea was in one of the cupboards. She knew Carla had a liking for the premier tea and hoped she'd find a few bags. After a brief search, she found the treasured packages.

She was taking her first sip when Troy entered the room.

He stopped at the entrance, a lopsided grin on his face. Desire, hot and sweet, coursed through her body. She struggled to breathe properly, slowly counting to ten and willing her body under control.

"The tea is ready," she said, placing her teacup down. "And there is some chocolate cake. Would you like a slice?"

She hoped her attempt at being cool and polite would work at keeping her desire at bay.

He stepped forward to stop at the kitchen island where she sat, pulled out a stool, and sat across from her. "Yes, you know I can't resist anything sweet," he replied, though the way he looked at her made her feel hot and bothered.

She didn't respond. Instead, she stood and moved toward the counter and cut a generous slice of the cake for him. She returned to her seat and set the plate down before him, sighing in relief at the distance between them.

*Good, he won't be able to touch me from there.*

Instead, his eyes remained fixed on her as if he were trying to look deep into her soul.

They were silent as they ate, but her awareness of him threatened to consume her. She could feel the heat radiating from her body, warming her with its intensity.

"Thanks for taking us out today," she said. "The

kids really enjoyed themselves. I'm sure they'll sleep late tomorrow morning."

"Yes, they had a good time. And what about you?" he asked, his voice low and husky. "Did you have a good time?"

"Of course I did," she replied, trying to sound light and casual. "As long as the kids are happy I'm fine. Their moods are infectious."

"True. Can't see myself not having fun around them. Maybe one day, you'll have your own," he said.

"I'm sure that's not going to happen anytime soon," she replied. "I don't seem to have luck with men."

"So what's wrong with me? I'm a good catch."

"You are? I've been there and it would be crazy to go there again. Remember, you're not about commitment."

"Maybe I've changed," he hinted.

"Have you? Changed?"

He hesitated.

"That hesitation does say a lot," she said sarcastically. "I'll have to see the change to believe it."

"Maybe if you didn't try to avoid me whenever you're on the island, you'd see that I'm not that bad a person. Some women would consider me a good catch."

"I'm sure you're one of the island's most eligible bachelors, but with your work, you don't have any time for love, marriage or commitment."

"Okay, maybe you're right, but it's more about what I want for myself. I'm not averse to marriage or commitment. But do you think I should give up what I've worked so hard to achieve?"

"Why does it have to be giving up? Why can't it be part of your life? Wife, family and your career."

He internalized what she'd said before he replied.

"I'm not sure if we're going to come to any agreement with our views so conflicting. However, I'd like to ask a question."

She nodded.

"What do we do about this thing between us? I know that you can feel the heat every time you come near me."

"And that's all it is, Troy. Lust and nothing else. I'm liberal enough to admit I loved having sex with you. I'm not looking for commitment, so have no fear. I don't want to end up like my mother. I saw it happen in live, brilliant color, so I have no plans to go there. You doctors are all the same. You immerse yourselves in your work and the people in your life, the people you love, play second fiddle to the glory you get from healing people, from performing all those miracles that consume your lives."

"And the people in our lives end up being alone," he said. "Is that what you are trying to say?"

"It proves my point. Commitment is not for doctors."

He glanced down at his watch. "I think it's time I leave. I have a busy day tomorrow. You know, a miracle or two to perform," he said. She could tell she'd annoyed him. His words dripped with sarcasm.

She did not respond, only stared at him, seeing the unexpected hurt in his eyes.

He turned to go, but stopped in midstride. "What are your plans for the kids tomorrow?"

"We're staying in tomorrow, but I plan to take them to the beach later this week. I'm hoping you'll be willing to come. Just let me know when your next day off is and we can go. Don't want to take them to the beach on my own."

"That's smart. I'll let you know when I have another day I can take off. I'll drop by tomorrow," he said. "Thanks for the chocolate cake."

"Would you like another slice to take home?" she asked.

He smiled and said, "You know I can't refuse."

He took the cake from her, their hands touching, sparks filling the room.

"Come walk me to the door, so you can lock up after I go."

She followed him down the corridor and to the door, watching as he opened it and turned to her.

"Thanks again for the cake. I'll call tomorrow to let you know when I'm off again."

"Bye. Drive carefully."

He turned to leave and stopped in his tracks.

He stared at her, and with his free hand pulled her to him.

He lowered his head, his lips touching her in a kiss that sent bolts of lightning through her body.

The kiss was gentle, a touching of lips and the gentle probing of his tongue. It was sweet like honey, and he wanted to sip like a bee enjoying its first taste of pollen.

When his lips left her, she felt an unexpected sense of disappointment. She instinctively leaned forward, wanting to feel his touch again.

"And you pretend like you don't want me," he teased, a big grin on his face. "Sweet dreams. I'll be dreaming of you, too."

With that he turned and walked away, confidence in his swagger.

She touched her lips, still feeling the slight pressure of his.

He was right. She'd be dreaming of him tonight, of him and a sweet stolen kiss.

She closed the door behind him, activating the security code, her hands trembling so much she took a while to complete the task.

The kiss had left her aching for more. She wondered how long this game would continue between the two of them. She had no intention of giving in to him again, but a part of her knew that she was fighting a losing battle. Each time he touched her, she melted. The sexual awareness between the two of them still flamed red-hot.

She wanted him—there was no sense denying it. Even now, the heat within had surged downward and settled between her legs.

She was hot and flustered. She walked slowly back to the kitchen, quickly washing the dishes and cutlery in the sink and making sure she left the room spick-and-span. She was a stickler for cleanliness and knew she would probably make some man's life miserable with her neatness.

She headed upstairs, peeping in on the kids, who were fast asleep. When she reached her room, she stripped, headed to the bathroom and quickly took a shower.

Later, in bed, she could not sleep, thoughts of *him* still on her mind.

She forced him from her mind, trying to focus on the episode of *Fresh Prince* on TV Land, but nothing helped. She suspected that it would be a long time before she fell asleep.

A few miles away, Troy put the phone down and sighed in frustration. His talks with his mother always ended this way. He was amazed that after all these years, she continued to try matchmaking. He didn't like it, and despite his asking her to refrain, she paraded eligible bachelorette after bachelorette before him. He'd reached the stage when he no longer attended any of her dinners. He preferred to just drop by, but even then he was at risk of meeting one of her lady friends who, encouraged by his mother, would attempt to flirt outrageously with him.

He did plan on visiting her soon. He wanted to talk with her about her life. What Sandra had said to him about her mother made him wonder about his own mother's happiness.

He had no doubt that his father loved his mother, but he now wondered about her happiness. She always looked happy, but there were moments when he saw a flicker of sadness. She would quickly cover it with a smile that would light up the room, and he would wonder if he'd seen correctly.

From what he knew, his mother and father had

married early and he'd come along quite soon after their first anniversary. He could always remember his mother being there, always at home, always doing their bidding.

It had never ever crossed his mind that her life might be lacking, that she'd not fulfilled any of her own dreams. The thought alone made him sad.

He sighed. There was nothing he could do about it tonight, but he planned on talking to her soon.

He turned his thoughts away from his mother and headed upstairs to his bedroom. Entering the room, he stripped, allowing the clothes to fall to the floor. He picked them up and when he reached the bathroom, he dropped them in the clothes basket.

He stepped into the shower and turned the water on at full blast. Its coolness, along with its force, stung him, but he didn't adjust it. His body, already on fire, slowly cooled.

Sandra had done this to him. How many times had he tried to push her image from his mind? The kiss had shaken his usual equilibrium.

His slowly cooling body renewed with the heat of his wanting. His penis hardened, his erection taut and painful. Images of her flashed in his mind vivid and bold, and he did all he could to keep them at bay, but to no avail.

She'd captured him in the web of his imagination. He groaned. He was beginning to sound all poetic and romantic. This was all about sex, or it should be.

Was he changing?

He didn't know, but something unexpected and

strange was happening to him. And he didn't like it one bit.

Sandra was different from all the women he knew and had slept with. Despite her aversion to him, there were things about her he liked. She had a wonderful sense of humor and was great with the kids, and she did not have a problem with speaking her mind. He admired her honesty.

He felt…helpless, as if he were losing a part of himself that he could no longer call his own, could no longer control.

He turned the faucet off and stepped out of the shower.

He needed to sleep. Maybe tomorrow he'd feel differently. Maybe tomorrow he'd gain control of his life again.

Sandra Walters was to blame for all of this. He definitely needed to purge her from his mind.

As he lay his head on the pillow, he acknowledged the reality of his situation.

## Chapter 4

On Tuesday morning, Troy watched as his father closed the door behind him and entered his office.

His father smiled in greeting.

"Morning, son, I've been hearing some good things about you," his father said.

He wasn't sure what his father was talking about, but his chest swelled with pride. Maybe today was going to be a good one. He'd not thought about Sandra too often this morning. He'd made sure that he kept busy.

"I just left Dr. Craig's room. Since he's been appointed chief of medical staff, he's been observing the young doctors closely. He's convinced that you'll eventually be a great surgeon. He does believe that you're finally focused and committed to what you want. I'm glad to hear that. I was disappointed when you didn't accept that fellowship I went out of my way to get for you."

"I told you I didn't plan to go," Troy replied. "I don't want you to use your influence to get things for me anymore. There is *already* talk here that I've only achieved a lot of what I have because I'm your son."

"It's true. What's wrong with that? My name does mean something around here," his father responded.

He loved his father, but it was at times like these when he wondered why his father didn't just leave things alone.

"I don't think you understand what I mean. I've tried to explain before that I want to make it on my own. I appreciate what you did for me when I was younger, but now I have to prove that I can do it on my own merit. I don't want to always be wondering if I've achieved what I have only because of my father."

"If that's the way you want it, I'll let you do it your way. All it means is that you'll take longer to achieve what you want. You've always been too stubborn."

"Dad, don't talk to me like that. I'm not a little boy. Damn, I love you, but you have to start treating me like an adult."

The look on his father's face was priceless. His father paused for a moment as if he couldn't believe his son had spoken to him like that. Then he smiled, that wonderful big smile that Troy loved.

"I'm sorry, son," his father finally said. "I didn't realize that my enthusiasm affected you like this."

His father walked around his desk, coming to stand

behind him. He stood, allowing his father to put his arms around him.

"Why haven't you ever said how you feel before? I *have* been really hard on you these past few years, haven't I? I didn't mean to intrude on your life. I only wanted to help, but I realize I can be a bit overpowering at times."

"It's okay, Dad. No harm done. I just want to make some decisions on my own."

"And I understand. Why didn't you tell me this before? I didn't realize I was embarrassing you. On reflection, I should have realized that you'd be under a lot more pressure because I'm your father."

"Dad, it's fine," he responded. "You didn't embarrass me."

"I did come to tell you something else," his father said, finally releasing him and returning to stand in front of the desk. "I talked to your mom about it and she is completely in agreement."

"Not another date for me?"

"No." His father laughed. "Your mother just wants the best for you, but I'll talk to her. She's a bit like me. We just need to remember that you are your own man now."

"So what is it?" Troy asked, all sorts of possibilities flashing in his head. He hoped neither of them was ill.

"I'm retiring at the end of the month," his father said. "I sent in my papers a few weeks ago. I could have gone a few years ago, but I didn't. Now I realize I don't want to spend the rest of my life here. I want to focus the rest of my years on your mother. She deserves my time now. I love her more than I did when I met her that day so many years ago, and her devotion to me has been unwavering. Maybe we'll take that trip around the world she's always fantasized about. Whatever she wants, I'll give her."

"Sounds like a good idea. I'll be sorry to see you go."

"I know, but I agree with you. It *is* time I move on and let you grow. You don't need me anymore."

"Oh, Dad, that's not true. I still need you and Mom. You've always been there for me. It's going to be hard not having you around here. Means I'm going to have to drop by the house more often."

"Good, your mother will love that," his father said, laughing. "Im sure she has a new girl lined up for inspection," he continued, chuckling.

"Oh, God."

"I don't know if I agree with her matchmaking, but I do want to have some grandchildren while I'm still strong and healthy."

"I'll see what I can do," Troy replied. He stood up, coming from behind the desk to stand by his father.

"I'm happy for you, Dad."

"Then all is good between us." His father hugged him again, one of those strong bear hugs that somehow made him feel as if he was ten years old again and everything was going to be all right.

"Thanks, Dad," he said as his father pulled away.

"You're my son and I love you. No thanks needed. You know, I may not have said this often enough, but I'm proud of you. I couldn't have wanted a better son.

And don't forget you haven't bought your mother's birthday gift."

With that, his father turned and left.

Troy returned to his chair, and, for a while, he sat in silence.

The phone rang, breaking the silence. Before he disconnected the call, he was hurrying out of his office. There'd been a serious accident on the highway and he was needed for surgery.

Ten minutes later, scrubs on, he entered the operating room. Like each time he stood before a patient, it was a matter of life and death. For the sake of the four-year-old girl he was about to operate on, he was determined that it was going to be life.

Two hours later, he stepped out of his scrubs and rested his head against his locker. He was weary, every bone in his body ached, but he felt a happiness that threatened to make him cry. He'd saved that little girl's life. He knew that she would rally through the next few days. She'd survive. He knew it.

Days like this made him more and more convinced that he was taking the right direction with his life; that going after his dreams could never be wrong. He wasn't doing it for his father. He was doing it for his patients.

Each time he performed a successful surgery, he felt a rush so strong that it gave validation to what he did. He never failed to embrace his talent. He admittedly was not the most religious individual but he did go to church on occasion. He never failed to thank God for the talent He'd given him. He assumed that since he was using his gift wisely, God would forgive him for the occasional lapse in judgment.

He dressed quickly before heading to the waiting room to let the girl's parents know how she was doing. He dreaded this part of his job, even when it was good news. He preferred to work with patients, to offer them comfort. The other tasks were just window dressing, an aspect of his job that was necessary.

The parents, as expected, were all teary-eyed and emotional. The mother hugged him as if she didn't want to let go.

An hour later, his day finally at an end, he glanced down at his watch. It was almost seven o'clock and he'd promised Sandra and the children he'd be over.

He straightened up his desk and left his office, the quickening of his heartbeat indicating the excitement he was feeling.

He drove quickly. He wanted to see the kids…and Sandra. He wondered what they were doing. Maybe relaxing, maybe playing. It didn't matter. He just needed to see her.

Sandra glanced at the clock for the hundredth time. It was almost eight o'clock. Where was he? Didn't he realize he had a duty to the kids? They'd asked for him several times. She wondered if something was wrong. But no, she was sure someone, George or Tamara, would call and let her know.

Maybe he had to work late or had an emergency. He could have called and let her know that something was wrong. Didn't he realize the kids would worry?

She glanced down at the floor where Darius and Lynn-Marie lay among heaps of pillows, their eyes focused on the latest Disney movie, *The Princess and the Frog*.

For a while she'd enjoyed the antics of the animated frogs as they traveled across the New Orleans bayou. Now she could not help but wonder.

She stopped. She'd heard a noise. The doorbell rang and then she heard the rattling of keys. Troy.

"Sandra." She heard his voice in the distance.

She stood, moving to the door and shouted a response. "We're in the entertainment room."

His heavy footsteps heralded his approach. Her hands trembled. The excitement of seeing him heightened her discomfort.

When he finally appeared, she stepped back, letting him enter, but not before she noticed how tired he looked.

As she'd suspected, it was his work.

He sat immediately, his body relaxing within the comfort of the sofa.

"You had a hard day?"

"Yes, I did, but I'm good. I saved a little girl's life today. I can deal with my fatigue."

Sandra heard the hint of pride in his voice. The work he did was so important. "I'm really glad it turned out well. How old is she?" Sandra asked.

"Four. The car her mother was driving was involved in an accident. She sustained serious head trauma, but I was able to take care of it. Her recovery will be slow, but I'm optimistic she'll make a full one."

"You must be proud of what you accomplished."

"It's all part of a day's work."

"I'm sure that's not all it means to you. You're not as indifferent as you pretend to be."

He shrugged.

"Auntie Sandra, the movie is finished. Can we have something to eat?"

"I'll make some sandwiches. Since we ate dinner early, I knew you'd want a snack before you went to bed. You stay and chat with Uncle Troy."

She didn't have to say it. Lynn-Marie was already sitting comfortably in Troy's lap while Darius was telling him all about the movie they'd just watched.

In the kitchen, she prepared a full plate of sandwiches, sure to add lots of peanut butter and jelly on the ones for the kids. She added another plate with cookies and placed them on a tray with four cans of soda.

When she returned to the room, *Ice Age 2* was already showing, so she passed out the sandwiches and joined them on the floor. Of course she found herself sitting next to Troy, his head resting on two pillows.

His eyes were closed. He was so tried. She wondered why he hadn't called and gone straight home but immediately knew it was because he wouldn't shirk his responsibility to the children.

She touched him and his eyes opened.

"Here are your sandwiches and a can of soda. Sprite, right?"

"You remembered?"

"Yeah, I remembered."

"Thanks," he replied. "I feel like I could eat a horse. Literally."

"Sorry, I don't have any available," she teased. "Just let me know if you want anything else. I hope you ate at work?"

"I didn't get a chance to."

"So you haven't eaten all day?" she asked.

"Just breakfast this morning. But I always make sure I have a good one in case I have an emergency like the one I had today. I don't always get the chance to eat."

"You should have told me that. I would have made something more substantial than a sandwich. I could warm up the pasta leftover from dinner."

"If it's not too much trouble, but I'll have the sand-wich. I can get something more when I get home."

"Uncle Troy, you really want to eat a whole horse?" Lynn-Marie asked, her expression one of disbelief. "You must be really hungry."

"You can have some of my sandwich," Darius said, breaking his in two.

"Thanks, Darius. Your Auntie Sandra is going to get me some pasta."

"Oh, meatballs and spaghetti. It was so good. Aunt Sandra can cook better than Mommy."

"Darius, you don't let your mom hear you say that," Sandra admonished.

"I won't, but she knows. I hear her tell Dad all the time that cooking is a drag."

"If she says so." Sandra stood. "I'll go get the pasta for your Uncle Troy. Just need to pop it in the microwave."

When she returned fifteen minutes later, it was to find the three of them sprawled on the floor and fast asleep.

She touched Troy again, waking him immediately.

"You can eat. I'll take the kids up to their room."

"No, just let me take Darius up. I can eat when I come back down. He's already in his pajamas."

After making sure Lynn-Marie was settled, Sandra returned to the room. Troy was already there, the plate almost empty.

He looked up. "Darius was right. You're a good cook. This is heavenly."

"Thanks," she replied, sitting next to him on the floor but making sure she was not too close.

"You've saved me from passing out. I have to be at work early in the morning. I'm working from tomorrow until Thursday. Maybe we can do something with the kids on Friday?"

"I'll ask them if there's anywhere in particular they'd like to go."

"Sounds fine to me. Shayne and Carla return on Saturday and I leave for St. Vincent on Sunday. I have a few surgeries to perform there."

"You must be very good to be invited by another country to perform surgeries."

"I've never looked at it that way. I just saw it as a job I had to do."

"For someone who's so concerned about his dream, you have a strange disregard for your accomplishments."

He shrugged but didn't reply. He continued to eat in silence. When he was done, he laid the fork on the plate and stood. "I am proud of what I've accomplished, but I see no need to boast about what I do. That my patients live is what's important to me.

"I'm sorry to have to leave as soon as I've eaten, but I'm really tired and need to get some sleep. I have to be at work at 7:00 a.m."

"No problem. Just leave everything there and I'll do the cleaning up."

"Not walking me to the door?"

"I wasn't planning to. I'll make sure the door is locked before I go up. I think the door locks when it's closed. I'm sure I'll be safe until I activate the system."

"Okay, you have a good night. And don't think that because you've escaped tonight, it won't happen again."

"Escape?" she asked, her eyes lit with bewilderment, and then her face flushed red. She understood exactly what he meant. "I really don't appreciate your toying with me. If that's what you do with your little floozies, fine, but you definitely won't use me as another notch on your bedpost."

He smiled knowingly. "My darling Sandra, your notch is already there."

"You dawg!" She moved swiftly toward him, raising her hand to slap him.

He grabbed her wrist, holding it firmly.

"The last woman to slap me in my face regretted it. Don't think it'll turn out like those soap operas on TV...not that kissing that delicious mouth of yours isn't tempting."

For a moment they struggled. "I think I'm going to kiss you anyway."

"You won't dare!"

He dared. His mouth captured hers and he slipped his tongue inside, her ready groan belying her protest.

"Now I'm convinced you want me." His lips left hers, leaving her aching for more. "You don't know how much you tempt me into taking you right here and now, but I'll take my time. When you come to me the next time, I want you willing and aching."

"Don't be presumptuous," she reported. "I don't want you."

He moved closer to her, causing her to tremble. With every breath she took, she wanted him, but she'd never admit it to him.

She loved it; she hated it, this passion that he stirred in her, causing her to ache for his touch.

He smiled finally.

"I'm heading home. Sweet dreams."

She didn't answer. She just stood watching him as he left.

*Sweet dreams, my ass.* How on earth could she have sweet dreams after he left her all frustrated and flustered?

Her dreams would more likely be salacious.

She had no doubt that he would enter her dreams as he did each night.

*Yeah, sweet dreams, my ass!* She hoped that he had his own dreams.

Troy entered the quiet of his home and for the first time felt that he wanted more. The silence he'd once embraced and relished pressed down on him like an ominous darkness. He closed the door behind him, stifling the urge to run back out and return to the Knight Plantation.

His common sense told him that going back would place him in a situation he didn't want.

He'd always felt so in control of his love life, but things were changing. Feelings he'd not experienced before seemed to be toying with his emotions.

He walked along the hallways, switching the lights on. He dropped his briefcase in the study and then headed for the stairs. He was tired, and the best thing he could do would be to get a good night's sleep.

He glanced at the tiny calendar on his bureau. Shayne and Carla would return soon. He couldn't believe that in four days, the cruise would be over and the children wouldn't need him anymore.

A feeling of dread washed over him. Was he getting soft? The thought of not being with the kids scared him.

In that moment, he had an epiphany. He wanted what Shayne had. He wanted a wife and a house filled with the laughter of children who didn't have a care in the world.

He wanted a woman he could call his own.

He shook his head.

It was Sandra Walters who had him in this state of disquietude, and it made him uncomfortable.

He would spend Friday and Saturday with her and the kids, but after that he'd be heading on his way. He'd go to St. Vincent and, hopefully, stay there until she left the island.

Maybe if he called George, his friend would help him to see reason again.

He glanced at the clock. It was just after ten o'clock. George should be at home, unless he was out partying. He remembered those days when he and George, and sometimes Shayne, would be out all night. With Shayne, it had not been often, since he had been busy raising his younger brother and sister. Ironically, all of them were already married and living happily ever after.

He and George seemed to be the only ones not bitten by the bug.

He picked up the phone, dialing George's number automatically. George picked up immediately, but the voice on the line didn't sound too happy.

"George. It's Troy."

"Man, what're you doing calling me so late? I'm in bed."

"In bed? So early? It's just after ten, and on a Tuesday night. I thought you'd be at the Ship Inn as usual."

"Troy, I know you think I'm the world's biggest party animal. I keep telling you, I'm not like that anymore. I've changed."

"Changed? What the hell are you talking about?" He laughed loudly.

"If you're going to laugh at me, I'm going to put the phone down. And after waking me from sleeping."

"Are you sick?"

"I'm fine, Troy. I just need some rest. That trial is

coming up and I'm not sure if I'm ready for what's going to happen."

"The Donovan case?" Troy asked.

"Yes," George responded.

"I'm sure you'll be happy to have it over and done with."

"You can't imagine." George stopped. "We'll talk sometime tomorrow."

"What are you doing on Saturday? You can come over and hang out with us. Your godchildren have been asking for you."

"Sure, I'm free this weekend. Shayne told me you'd be babysitting. Of course, I wasn't invited to help take care of them—you're the responsible one. And how are you enjoying the delectable Sandra Walters?"

Troy didn't respond.

"Cat got your tongue?" George teased. "I don't know why the two of you don't just admit you love each other and get married."

"I suggest you go back to sleep. I'll expect to see you on Saturday."

"Cool. I'll definitely come over on Saturday."

"We'll plan something special for the kids."

"Ok, I'll bring over some food and a movie or two."

"Good, I'll let Darius know. You know he's totally devoted to you."

"I know. Sorry to cut the call short. I really need to get some sleep."

"Cool, bro."

He listened for the click before he put the phone down. He would talk to George soon or wait until Shayne returned. He definitely needed someone to talk to. He needed to sort out his thoughts.

He wanted time to stop. For his life to be like it used to be. Not complicated. He wanted to focus on his goal. Wanted to focus on the things that were important to him.

But what were those things? He wasn't sure what he wanted anymore.

Sandra was too much of a temptation for him, and she insisted that she had no desire to indulge in anything he had to offer. If he wanted to bed her again, he had a hard job ahead of him. She got right under his skin. He knew that if he made love to her again he would never want to stop, and that was reason enough to stay away from her.

An hour later, he sat on the balcony outside his bedroom, no less confused than he had been when he'd first laid eyes on Sandra Walters.

A few miles away, Sandra sat watching Lynn-Marie sleep. Moments like these always left her feeling… empty. There was something so precious about watching the little bundle of energy sleep.

Sandra was still amazed at the way Lynn-Marie played and played. Of course, having a brother with an equal amount of energy didn't help. They were wonderful kids—independent, lively and confident— but they knew they had boundaries and never threw tantrums when they didn't get what they wanted. For that she was grateful. She couldn't deal with spoiled brats.

At times, she wondered what it would be like to have a family of her own. She had wished for that with Peter, but he'd betrayed her, and the emotional scars still remained from the pain he'd inflicted.

There was a part of her that had wanted it all—a beautiful lace gown in the purest white silk, a sultry honeymoon and her fairy-tale ending.

Troy came to mind. There was no denying that he was a good man. She wanted him, wanted more, but there was no assurance that he could give her what she wanted.

Even though she often denied it, she was coming to the realization that the occasional romp between the sheets left her feeling cold.

She did want Troy to see her as more than a mere booty call.

She slipped off her clothes and slid between the sheets.

Tonight, she planned on having a good night's sleep...no heated dreams, no images of a sweaty, naked Troy. But as she drifted off, she knew he'd come as he did every night.

Her body shivered in anticipation.

## Chapter 5

In the early hours of the morning, heavy rain beat on the rooftop, waking Sandra with its pounding.

Sandra stretched, working the aching kinks from her body. Three days had passed since he'd kissed her. Whenever she thought of him, her body still tingled with the memory of his touch.

Troy had been busy at work, but each night he'd called and chatted briefly with the kids. Last night, he'd called and told her that today he'd be taking them on a picnic. She wondered if the kids were up yet, but suspected they weren't. Lynn-Marie would be already asleep next to her. The tiny tot had a habit of trotting into her room as soon as she woke up. She'd climb onto the bed, cuddle up against Sandra and proceed to fall back off to sleep.

As if on cue, there was a gentle knock on the door and a smiling Lynn-Marie appeared. She crossed over to the bed, climbed up and hugged Sandra before placing her head on Sandra's chest.

"I miss Mommy," she mumbled, "but I love you, Auntie Sandra, so I don't miss her so much." With that she closed her eyes and was soon fast asleep.

Tears filled Sandra's eyes, but she wasn't sure how else to respond. The child's words had touched her more than she could have imagined. In her own way, Lynn-Marie was trying to tell her that she was glad she was here.

An ache in her heart increased until she felt its physical manifestation. Oh, how she longed for the day she had her own child.

As expected, the image of Troy came immediately to mind in the form of a little boy with black hair and brown eyes.

She laughed. She must be crazy to imagine children of hers taking after Barbados's official confirmed bachelor. There was no hope for anything beyond the casual connection that had been forged between them. Nothing would happen between them again. She would have to say it out loud until she believed it.

There was another knock at the door and Darius's head appeared.

"Can I come in, Auntie Sandra?" he asked sleepily.

"Of course. Come lie next to me," she replied, patting the space on her left side. "I'm glad for the company."

Darius climbed up on the bed and lay next to her.

"Okay, I'm going back to sleep," he said, snuggling close to her.

"Me, too," she said, placing her arms around him.

"What are we doing today?"

"We're going on a picnic."

"With Uncle Troy?" he asked.

"Yes, with Uncle Troy."

"Oh, that's cool," he mumbled, almost asleep.

"Yeah, it's cool," she replied.

She watched as he drifted into sleep. They would be up in another hour or two. She'd sleep for a bit, too, and then go down to make breakfast.

She closed her eyes, willing herself to sleep, with the image of Troy on her mind.

When she woke an hour later, the rain had stopped. The kids were still fast asleep.

She slipped from the bed, unwinding the kids' arms from around her. She walked to the window, pulling the curtain apart.

The sun shone brightly, its smiling roundness just peeping from below the horizon. The rain had left its mark, the plants and trees sparkling fresh and vibrant.

She closed the curtains, not wanting the sun to wake the kids. She slipped into her robe and headed downstairs.

It was Thursday, two days before Shayne and Carla returned. A wave of regret filled her. She'd enjoyed living on the plantation, and the thought of going back to the U.S. made her feel a bit down. However, with the problem of Troy, maybe going back would be for the better. She'd stay on for another two weeks and then she would be gone. Fortunately, Troy would be in St. Vincent, so she'd be able to enjoy her holiday without being flustered by his presence.

In the kitchen, she stirred up a batch of pancakes and placed them in the microwave until the kids came downstairs. When that was done, she sliced fruit and made tropical fruit salad. She added tuna sandwiches, the kids' favorite, and took bottles of fruit juice from the pantry.

In an hour, she'd prepared all they needed for their picnic.

After she was done, she went upstairs and woke the kids. After quick baths, they headed downstairs to have breakfast.

Afterward she, along with the kids, sat on the veranda reading. Troy had promised he would come for them around midday.

She was looking forward to the outing. They were going to a park in the north of the island and then to a nearby animal sanctuary called the Wildlife Reserve.

Hopefully, she'd show him the kind of life he could have.

A few minutes after midday, Troy's SUV came up the driveway. Sandra was relieved. The kids were driving her crazy. Every five minutes they asked for the time. She understood their excitement. They were looking forward to the picnic, and she couldn't blame them. The day was perfect for picnicking. No evidence of rain remained. The sun smiled down directly overhead and the wonderful tropic breeze made its way across the island from the Atlantic Ocean to the east.

Half an hour later, they were driving northward on the ABC Highway. In the backseat, Lynn-Marie and Darius were singing songs from their favorite Disney movies. Next to her, Troy, with his deep baritone, joined in the impromptu sing-along.

Sandra was more than aware of Troy sitting next to her. Each time the car turned a corner, his leg pressed against hers. Bolts of heat raced through her body, but she chose to ignore it, trying to make sure he could not sense her reaction.

For the duration of the drive, she joined in the singing, trying to keep her voice cheerful. She knew Troy felt the sexual tension; his own body betrayed his discomfort and awareness of her proximity, in the rigid way he sat.

When they pulled into the Farley Hill National Park twenty minutes later, Sandra nearly leaped out of the car. The confines of the automobile and his closeness had been a bit too much to handle.

Fluffy clouds floated daintily across the crystal-clear blue sky. A cool breeze wafted across the island's eastern coast, stirring the leaves of the mahogany trees that had found their home in the park. Birds sung in harmony as if lauding the peacefulness of the surroundings.

Darius and his sister raced up and down the gently sloping hill that led to a tiny gazebo.

A pair of butterflies drifted by, and Lynn-Marie

screamed with excitement. She raced after the delicate winged things, her joy evident in her beaming smile.

"Come, Darius, come help me catch the butterfly!" she squealed.

Darius joined her and for several minutes, they dodged here and there, trying to catch one. Eventually, they gave up, drifting back to where Sandra and Troy sat on one of the two picnic blankets Troy had spread on the ground.

"This is the most wonderful day," Lynn-Marie said, hugging Sandra as she said it.

"Thanks for playing cricket with me, Uncle Troy," Darius said. "You can still bowl well for your age."

Sandra laughed.

"And what's that supposed to mean?" Troy asked Darius.

"You're better than Dad, and both of you are the same age," he said with the innocence of a child. "I'm tired."

Sandra glanced at Lynn-Marie, who had already nodded off.

"That's fine," she replied. "You take a rest."

Darius sprawled himself on the blue blanket, closed his eyes and was soon fast asleep.

This was the moment she had not been looking forward to. Being around Troy with the children awake had made things easier. They'd acted as a buffer for the whole day. Now that they'd fallen asleep, things would change; she'd be forced to confront him.

When she turned to him to say something, she noticed that he, too, had lowered himself to the ground and had fallen asleep.

She smiled and decided to join them. She closed her eyes and allowed herself to drift off to the sound of the wind whispering to the trees.

That evening, back at the plantation, Sandra kissed the already sleeping child and smiled down at her. The bundle of energy had once again given in to her fatigue.

She turned the lights off and exited the room, heading downstairs to the living room.

Troy was already sitting on one of the sofas. Her heart knocked against her ribs. His eyes flamed with desire. Truth be told, she could not deny her mood, and she knew that if he were to take her in his arms right now, it wouldn't take long for them to end up in bed. In fact, she suspected that that was where they would end up that night. The tension between them sizzled, powerful and potent.

She walked slowly into the room.

"I think I should be going," he said.

"I don't mind if you stay for a while," she replied. Why had she said that? "It's good to have an adult around, especially when you spend most of your time with children."

"You need some adult conversation?"

"Yes."

For a while he was silent, and like her, she knew he was locked in his thoughts. There was an uncertainty about the next word, about the next move. Sexual tension hovered in the air.

"Come with me on the balcony. So we can talk."

The last thing she wanted to do was talk, but maybe it was the best thing to do.

She wanted him, but maybe now wasn't the time. However, it felt like now or never. She knew it and he knew it. She could tell in the rigidity of his body.

Sandra moved slowly toward him, throwing caution to the wind.

She stopped when she reached him and looked deep into his dark eyes, noting the flames there. What else she saw there surprised her. He seemed vulnerable, uncertain. She'd never seen Troy as that kind of man. He always seemed so confident and sure of himself, especially that first night they'd made love.

She reached her hands up, holding his face between her palms before she pulled him toward her. Her lips touched his tentatively, as if giving him a chance to pull away. He hesitated briefly before capturing her lips with his. He kissed her long and hard as if desperate to taste her, as if their lack of intimacy had left him starved.

Despite its intensity, the kiss comforted her with its tenderness, something that seemed at odds with the heat between them.

His tongue slipped between her teeth, finding her own tongue where he suckled gently. She tasted the freshness of peppermint.

One of the things Sandra remembered about the first time they'd made love was the way he kissed her. He could kiss. She felt a bolt of red-hot lightning rush to the core of her femininity. She wanted him to make love to her, wanted to feel him deep inside her.

"Come to my room," Sandra said. He could feel her need.

"The guest room?" he asked.

"Yes," she replied, her voice husky with desire.

He lifted her easily. He loved holding her, especially the luscious curve of her buttocks.

At the top of the stairs, he turned right, making the short trek before he allowed her to stand.

Inside, he switched the lights on and gently lay her on the bed.

He looked down at her, her appearance innocent and wanton at the same time.

He lowered himself until his body pressed gently against her.

Sandra placed her arms around him, drawing him even closer until he could feel the firmness of her nipples against his chest. He shifted slightly, allowing him access to her upper body. He deftly unbuttoned the dress she wore and, when she stood, helped her out of it.

With a skill he'd developed during years of practice, he slipped her bra off, exposing two of the most luscious breasts he'd ever seen. He wanted to taste them. He lowered his head, using his mouth to take one turgid nipple between his teeth, and teased it until it became hard and taut with his ministration.

Beneath him, she groaned softly, her eyes closed, her face contorted with pleasure. He suckled on one sensitive peak and then the other, feeling her body trembling beneath his.

He moved his mouth downward, allowing his tongue to trail below her breasts and then down to her stomach, where his lips found the soft down covering her womanhood. He nuzzled there, hearing her laughter.

When he separated the velvet folds and plunged his tongue in, she gasped, her legs closing instinctively around his head. He continued, his tongue finding the sensitive nub. He tasted her, the sweet musky tang that heightened his need for her.

He moved briefly, fishing in his pants for one of the condoms he'd placed in his wallet.

He slipped it on, all the while his gaze linked with her now-opened eyes.

He shifted her on the bed, placing her between his legs as she surrendered.

Her legs parted, giving him access to the core of her womanhood. He placed his penis at the entrance, allowing her to adjust to his largeness. He entered her slowly, luxuriating in the feel of her tightness around him.

He stroked her slowly but firmly, his hips moving backward and forward in a motion that caused her to wrap her legs around him. Her body started to move in response to his gyrations, matching his with a force of her own.

This time, her eyes were open wide, fixed on his face as he worked his magic. It was a strange thing. During lovemaking, most of his lovers never looked at him during intercourse, as if they were embarrassed at what they were doing.

With Sandra, it felt right, different. From their first time, she'd experienced their lovemaking to the fullest. She'd been a full participant in their coming together. As he stroked her, she looked fully into his eyes as if searching to find something there.

One of the things he loved about her was her lack of inhibitions. She urged him on, whispered naughty things in his ears that heightened his sexual excitement.

"Don't stop," she gasped, her hands gripping his buttocks. "Harder, harder, harder," she urged him on. "I love you inside me."

He obliged her, increasing his speed and stroking her hard and fast.

Troy felt his body tense and knew his orgasm was imminent. He slowed his movement, wanting to extend their lovemaking, but it was too late. His body shuddered and every muscle contracted, bringing that pleasure-pain that came with the sweetness of release.

He groaned loudly, the intensity causing his abs to contract.

Under him, Sandra's own release was evident. She moaned loudly, her legs tightening around him, the walls of her vagina contracting and releasing around his penis.

He rolled over, pulling her body with his so she could lie on top of him. Her breathing was still coming sharp and short, but Troy could tell she was trying to regain control as he was.

For minutes, the only sound was their ragged

breathing. Her head rested against his chest and he could hear the heavy pounding of her heart.

In time, her breathing slowed and he heard a sigh before she spoke.

"Now that's what I call lovemaking," she purred, running a finger across his lips.

He laughed in reply, her comment unexpected. He caught her finger between his teeth, nipping it slightly. She shivered in response.

"My sentiments exactly. We're good for each other."

She didn't respond.

"No comment?" he finally asked.

"I'm not sure what to say. Yes, we are attracted to each other, but you are not looking for commitment and I have this…thing about doctors."

"So I'm the bad doctor?" he asked. After what they'd just shared, he felt somewhat offended.

"Do I need to answer that?" she replied.

"I can understand being angry with your father and ex-fiancé, but all doctors?"

"Most doctors I know personally are too cavalier about relationships, you included."

"I wouldn't say I'm cavalier about relationships. I've respected every woman I've slept with. We were all consenting adults. I see nothing wrong with what I've done. Did you want more out of what we have?"

She hesitated before she replied, "No, I didn't expect anything else."

He glanced at her, a frown on his face. He glanced down at his watch.

"I think it's time I go. Don't forget that George and I

are taking you all out on Saturday. We'll make a day of it and be back in time for Shayne and Carla's arrival."

He pulled her to him and kissed her, a slow, desperate kiss that made her ache to have him again, but she controlled her need and did nothing when he ended the kiss and moved away.

"I may not be the kind of person you admire, but I'm a good man. I've never thought of commitment before. Maybe because I've not met the right person. Maybe because I haven't wanted anyone to intrude on my dreams. However, I see you in a different light. I respect you, and maybe you're the one who's going to shake my world and make me think of happily ever after. Don't you think we deserve to allow ourselves the chance?"

She looked at him steadily. "Okay, maybe you're right. I'm just not open for being hurt by another doctor."

"So what happened to you and your fiancé?" he asked, curiosity getting the better of him.

"I'd prefer not to talk about it right now."

"Cool, I respect your wishes. But we will talk." He stood to leave.

She watched as he walked away, wondering what she'd gotten herself into.

Maybe she was doing the right thing giving him a chance. She could not deny that she was immensely attracted to him. It went further—each time she saw him, she wanted him more. It was not that she'd never had lovers before. She'd had several lovers, but she'd always made sure that there had been some sort of commitment to the relationship. She'd entered most to fulfill a need for companionship and the intimacy of a lover.

With Troy, it was different.

Tonight, she'd annoyed him, but she'd apologized. She hoped it wasn't too late to make amends.

At home, Troy did what he did each night. He thought about Sandra. The woman had worked herself under his skin, and he wasn't sure where this would all end.

As he lay in bed, he remembered all the things he'd said to her and realized that a lot of what he'd said had been in the moment. It was better leaving her on her own. Tomorrow would be the last day of taking care of the kids and then he'd be free of her.

He noticed his phone blinking and wondered who'd left a message. Why hadn't the person called on his cell? And then he remembered he'd forgotten his cell at home.

He picked the phone up, punched in his password at the voice prompt and listened to his only message. Dr. Craig needed him to work on Saturday. A seriously injured patient was being flown into the island the next day with the surgery scheduled for Saturday. He wouldn't have to see Sandra tomorrow, and the day after that, he'd be off to St. Vincent. He'd call in the morning, apologize and then he'd be free of her.

A wave of sadness washed over him, but he refused to succumb to his unexpected moment of vulnerability.

This was for the better.

Having Sandra in his life was a bit more complicated than he'd expected. Unexpected feelings were coming in to play, leaving him feeling that he was no longer in control.

He glanced at the clock. Three o'clock. He needed to get some sleep. He was tired. Maybe tonight he'd sleep deep enough that a sexy, buxom temptress would not invade his dreams.

## Chapter 6

When George finally arrived on Saturday, with no Troy in sight, Sandra suspected that he wouldn't be coming. Unlike her, the kids weren't upset by his absence. Their "Uncle George" was a great substitute.

While Troy was the more serious type, George was funny, flirtatious and spontaneous. However, despite his sexy good looks and charm, George failed to stir her in the way Troy did.

It wasn't his personality; it wasn't that he wasn't an eloquent conversationalist. It wasn't even because she was taller than he was. At just under her five-foot-seven height, George was short, but what he lacked in height, he made up for in stature.

He was all rippling muscles, and each time Sandra

saw him, she wondered if a master sculptor had carved him to perfection.

He was definitely sexy. His reputation as a playa preceded him, and not in a bad way. His buddies poked fun at him constantly. However, George took their ribbing with a smile. He had a smile that could break a woman's heart, and Sandra was sure he'd broken many.

But he wasn't Troy, and that was the problem.

"Mornin'," George said, planting a kiss on her cheek and hugging her tightly.

"Where is Uncle Troy?" Darius asked.

"I'm sorry, he can't be here. He had to go to the hospital."

Sandra felt a surge of anger. He was avoiding her and didn't have anything to do at the hospital. She stared at George, who tried to avoid looking directly at her. He knew something, and she planned on asking him.

"Kids, go get your hats so we can leave," she told Lynn-Marie and Darius. The kids rushed inside in excitement.

As soon as they disappeared, she turned to George.

"Does he really have to go to the hospital?" she asked.

"That's something you'd have to take up with him," George replied. "He called me this morning and told me to let you know he couldn't make it, that he needed to go into work."

"I have no doubt it could be so. It's always about the job with doctors."

"Sandra, I assure you, it's not only about the doctors—it's also about their patients."

She had the good grace to feel a flash of shame and knew it showed.

"Sorry, I'm just a bit annoyed. The children will be disappointed."

"For a while, but they love their Uncle George just as much." He grinned, his large chest puffed up.

"That's true," she replied, and as if to confirm what she said, Darius and Lynn-Marie came flying out the door and came to an immediate halt.

"Haven't I told the two of you not to run in the house?" she chided. "You're going to hurt yourselves one day."

"Sorry, Auntie Sandra," they replied in unison, innocence on their faces. Of course, she noticed they didn't promise it wouldn't happen again.

"Well, I'm not going to say it again. The next time it happens, I'm going to take your television privileges away for a day. You won't want that, will you?"

"No," they both said.

"Good," she replied. She turned to George. "We're ready when you are."

Their reprimand already forgotten, the kids cheered and walked slowly to the car.

Sandra smiled at the effort to slow down. Maybe she was being a bit too strict, but she didn't want them to hurt themselves, especially Lynn-Marie.

She followed George. She was going to enjoy today. With or without Troy Whitehall. His absence was just proof that anything more between them was doomed for failure. They weren't even involved yet and he was missing dates. She knew she was being selfish. He was valuable to his patients, was one of the best in his field.

She needed to resolve this situation, but she was torn by the fear of dealing with a situation she had not only seen with her mother and father, but one she had dealt with when she was engaged. For doctors, their work and patients always came first. And while it all seemed honorable and noble, she didn't want a life of waiting and being alone.

Troy drove away from the hospital feeling as if he'd wasted the whole day. While he'd tried to focus on writing some long-overdue reports, his thoughts had been on Sandra and the kids. The thought of her spending the day with the ever-flirting George gave rise to a painful gnawing in the pit of his stomach, despite knowing George would never betray him.

But why would it matter if George was there or not? He didn't want her for himself, he had made this quite clear.

Maybe going over to a friend's home tonight was a good decision. When a friend, Keisha, had called during the day and invited him over for a nightcap he'd immediately accepted. Maybe this is what it would take to purge the doctor-hating Sandra from his mind. He and Keisha hooked up on occasion, but there was no attachment, just consenting adults having sex. He cringed at how clinical it sounded, but he was being honest.

He was accustomed to these spur-of-the-moment

calls from Keisha. She wanted sex, and he had no problems fulfilling her need.

On the drive over, he knew that something was seriously wrong. Usually, he'd be experiencing the anticipation of a few hours of hot, kinky sex. Keisha had very few inhibitions about lovemaking. He remembered clearly the time she encouraged him to have sex in her garden during the early hours of the morning, claiming that her next-door neighbor would be fast asleep.

The next morning, as he'd driven away, the elderly Mrs. Clarke had smiled sweetly and winked slyly at him. The thought still embarrassed him.

It had taken him almost two months before he had the courage to visit Keisha again. Of course, there were no more garden performances for Mrs. Clarke.

Even the thought of that wild, daring night did nothing to heighten his anticipation. Maybe when he saw her, his mood would change.

When he arrived at the house, he was greeted by a dominatrix in black with blood-red lips. His manhood refused to respond, and he knew that he could not go through with his plan.

When Keisha tried to initiate intimacy, he asked if he could eat first.

She complied, but when he tried to prolong dinner, her annoyance turned to confusion. He'd expected anger, not the look of genuine concern.

"We don't have to make love, you know," Keisha said.

He looked at her closely. He had not expected this

response. "I'm sorry," he said, reaching to hold her hands in his.

"Who is she?" she asked, her voice unusually soft and sad. "She must be important to have you this agitated. In all the time I've known you, you've never, ever refused sex. Not even when you were tired from a long surgery."

"Agitated? Me?"

"Yes, you. I could tell something was wrong from the moment you stepped through the door."

"It makes no sense denying it, does it?" he said.

"No, but I'd have to say she is one lucky lady."

"Who doesn't even want me? She doesn't like doctors! She thinks we're the scum of the earth."

"You're lovers?"

"Yes," he confirmed.

"Then she doesn't really think you're the scum of the earth," Keisha suggested. "If she did she wouldn't have made love to you."

"But she keeps pushing me away," he argued.

"And you haven't been doing the same thing?"

"Okay, maybe I have been. I'm not even sure how I feel about her. At times I feel as if I love her, and at other times, she gets me so annoyed. But I'm not sure if I'm interested in having a serious relationship. You know me. I'm all about my career and advancing up the ladder. It's not about the glory that comes with it. I just want to get better so I can help people, heal people."

"That's only a part of it. It's also about pleasing your father. He makes demands on you and you try to fulfill them to the detriment of who you are and what you want for yourself. It's strange when his marriage to your mother seems so solid that he doesn't want the same happiness for you. It just seems so selfish. At the end of the day, you'll be the one going home to an empty bed and coming by occasionally for some quick sex."

"You've never complained before," he retorted. Her words had struck too close to home.

"And I'm not complaining now. I know what I want for myself, but if I were in your shoes with the possibility of a forever, I'd give this up in the blink of an eye. You know what your real problem is?"

He didn't answer, just stared at her.

"You're afraid to love, so you use your career as an excuse. You don't even realize it. The only thing that will save you from yourself is a woman who loves you unconditionally. You just have to surrender to her embrace and all will be well. But men, they see things like these as weaknesses."

"This situation is so messed up, I don't even know my head from my ass. I feel so damn helpless at times. My life was uncomplicated and I was content until I met her. I didn't have all this craziness going on."

"Come, let's sit over here and you tell me all about this wonderful woman who has stolen your heart and whom you're hopelessly in love with." At his stern look, she modified her words. "Okay, not in love with yet. The woman who's slowly melting your heart and saving you from a lonely life."

She stood, taking his hand and leading him to the sitting room, where she pushed him onto a sofa and sat next to him. She guided his head to her lap, and while he described Sandra, she stroked his head gently, as a mother would do to soothe her child.

Soon, he stopped talking and she realized he'd fallen asleep. She shifted his legs onto the chair and placed a cushion under his head. She could tell he was tired. He was always tired.

She stood, her eyes on the beautiful man on her couch, while the pool of tears stung her eyes.

She knew this would be the last time he'd come here.

She turned away, a heavy sadness weighing her down. Maybe one day she'd find love. Despite her claim of independence, there was a part of her that had hoped that one day she'd find happiness with Troy.

Tonight, she knew that he'd never be hers.

He'd found love and didn't even realize it.

When Troy awoke, it was just before midnight. He glanced around, wondering where he was. Poor Keisha. He'd hurt her. Despite their unwritten agreement, he'd known that her feelings for him were deeper, but he'd chosen to ignore them.

Tonight, his admiration for her had increased two-fold. He'd seen a maturity and sensitivity that he'd not expected, that he'd not even realized she possessed. That was the sad thing. He didn't even know. He'd only seen her as someone who fulfilled a basic need, and for that he was sorry. He felt like a heel, and what made it worse was that he knew he would no longer come here.

He was in love. He didn't want to admit it, but he

was. He loved Sandra Walters and he knew he could no longer do anything about it.

However, it did not mean a happily-ever-after. Despite what George had told him, he knew that his life would only find fulfillment if he devoted it to helping people, and Sandra threatened his commitment to his job.

He could never see her committing to a relationship with him when he worked long hours. She had said that much.

Love, in this case, would not be enough.

He dressed quickly and was about to put his shoes on when he saw the fuchsia of a sticky note on one of his shoes. He picked it up and read: *You can only find true happiness when you reach for it.*

On the surface it seemed a typical cliché, but he realized that with those words she was letting him know that she was happy for him. She had often told him that if he ever decided not to visit her, she'd know that he'd moved on to someone better, someone more deserving of his love. He felt her sadness, but he also felt sad for her.

He moved toward her bedroom but changed his mind when he reached the door. The note had been her goodbye, and the woman she was would prefer it to end there. He would only be embarrassing her more by trying to talk and explain.

He looked around for a pencil, found one and wrote his own note on the back of hers.

*I hope you find what you want in life.*

A bit corny, but he really wished it for her. He hoped that someday she'd find happiness and contentment.

He looked around the room one last time, put the note by the telephone and left.

Half an hour later, he picked up the phone and dialed Shayne's number.

The phone was answered immediately.

"Why are you calling here so late? It's after midnight." Sandra's voice came over the line, angry and distant.

"I'm just calling to say I'm sorry for not making it today. I had to go to the hospital."

"It's fine, Troy. I didn't expect anything else. Remember, with you, work comes first. Thanks for calling and letting me know. I've already let the kids know you're sorry. With George around, they didn't think about you. We had a great time. I have to go. I need to get some sleep."

With that, he heard a click and she was gone.

Boy, she was angrier than he'd thought. It would be best to stay out of her way, and with him heading off to St. Vincent in a couple of days and Shayne and Carla returning the day before he left, it shouldn't be too difficult. Since she seemed to like George's company, the best thing to do would be to stay out of her way. By the time he returned from the neighboring island, she'd be gone.

And good riddance.

So how was it that the pain he felt seemed to physically hurt his heart?

* * *

Sandra slammed the phone down and suppressed the scream that threatened to fill the room. She breathed deeply. She didn't want to scare the kids, but if she went with her feelings, those around would think she'd gone crazy.

She turned the reading lamp off and snuggled into the covers. She felt calmer. Much calmer, and she lauded herself for her ability to come under control so soon.

To think he had the gall to call and apologize when he hadn't even had the decency to call her directly and let her know he'd not be coming.

While she had no doubt that he did go into work, she suspected that what he had to do was not an emergency. She was sure that if it had been, he would have told George the reason for his defection. That's what she thought of his being missing in action. Defection.

A coward who didn't want to face up to what was going on. He didn't even have the courtesy to drop by tonight and make his apologies in person. George had called him when they returned home and he hadn't answered his phone at home or his cell. He'd left work around six in the evening. Probably went to visit one of his floozies.

And as suddenly as her anger came, the tears started to flow. She tried to stop, but she couldn't.

And when she couldn't cry anymore, she closed her eyes and slept, a restless sleep that left her feeling miserable when she awoke in the morning.

\* \* \*

On Saturday night, Shayne and Carla finally returned, bearing gifts from their ports of call along the Mediterranean peninsula. Immediately, Carla noticed that something was not right. Sandra knew that before the night was over they'd have a talk, something she dreaded.

The knock on her door came that night after everyone had gone to bed.

Carla stepped inside, a look of genuine concern on her face.

"I won't waste time with pleasantries. What's going on?"

"Nothing," Sandra said, and then she stopped. There was no sense in lying to her best friend, especially after she'd prepared what she was going to say.

Instead, she started to cry.

Carla rushed over to the bed and sat, taking her in her arms.

"I know. Men are the worst kind of creatures, right?"

"Yes," Sandra replied between a sniffle and a snort.

"I'm assuming this is all about Troy?"

"Yes, he's a jerk," she mumbled.

"So you're going to tell me what's wrong?"

She inhaled deeply, trying to bring herself under control. Slowly, she lifted her head and stared Carla in the eyes.

"I haven't seen him since Friday night. He hasn't even called."

"And is there a reason why he's missing in action?" Carla asked, curiosity evident.

"Yes, I think he's angry with me."

"About what?"

She hesitated. "Our lovemaking."

"Your what?" Carla exclaimed. "So you've finally done it?"

"Yes, again."

"Again? What do you mean again? This has happened before?"

"Once."

"And I haven't heard about this! I thought we were best friends. You've never kept something like this from me before."

"I'm sorry, but this is all becoming so complicated. The first time was a long time ago. Your wedding night."

"My wedding night! So long ago? I can't believe this. Well, Shayne will be definitely happy about developments. We thought things had reached a bit of a standstill."

"So the two of you have been planning on getting us together?" she asked.

"No, not planning," Carla replied, shaking her head. "We were just hoping that something would develop. I know you were attracted to Troy from the time you met him, but you just have this irrational hang-up about doctors," she said. When Sandra opened her mouth to protest, she continued, "I know the reasons why."

When Sandra didn't respond she went on. "I'm not going to pick sides here, nor am I going to give you any profound advice. You're an adult and have to make up your own mind about this thing you and Troy have. My only suggestion is that you listen to your heart. Stop thinking so rationally and logically. Just let your heart lead."

She reached over and kissed Sandra on the cheek. "Now, I'm going to bed to cuddle up with my husband. I'm tired from all the sightseeing and lovemaking on the sea. When I left Shayne he was sleepy, thank God. Maybe, he'll let me get some rest tonight," she said, giggling like a schoolgirl in love.

"Thanks for not preaching to me. What you said is right. I'm the one who has to make the decision."

"I'm glad you realize that," Carla responded.

Sandra placed her arms around Carla and hugged her. "Thanks for being my friend."

"Oh, girlfriend, you know I love you. I just want to see you happy. And if it's not with Troy, true love will come to you when the time is right."

With that she kissed Sandra on her cheek and left.

Sandra sat silently on the bed, pondering what had just transpired.

What Carla had said was so true. She needed to forget all the illogical reasoning that kept her from dealing sensibly with Troy. She liked him, and from the first day she'd met him, she'd been bowled over by his handsome masculinity. There were so many aspects to his personality. At times he was funny, at others he was the serious, contemplative doctor, and then there were those times when he was the passionate, intense individual.

She didn't mean his passion when they made love. Yes, that was a part of it. It was his passion for his job, his patients, and the way he approached life. Under the generally serious facade, he was a man with an emotional intensity that surprised her.

Maybe if the opportunity arose again, she'd allow herself more.

Maybe if she allowed herself to see him as a hot-blooded man, instead of just a doctor, she'd see more, much more.

Unfortunately, she'd lost out on the opportunity to do this. By the time he returned to Barbados, she'd be gone.

## Chapter 7

Shayne and Sandra sat facing each other, engaged in their ongoing battle for chess supremacy. Carla rushed into the room.

"Shayne, I think we have to take Darius and Lynn-Marie to the doctor." She turned to Sandra. "I'm sorry, honey. It looks a lot like chicken pox. I've confined the kids to their rooms until we take them to the doctor. By this evening, we'll be sure what's the best thing to do. Hopefully, they haven't passed it on to you yet. Fortunately, both Shayne and I've had it."

"I haven't had it," Sandra replied. "It's really not a problem. I've probably caught it already."

"While that may be possible, I don't want to take that chance," Carla replied. "Makes no sense spoiling your holiday if you don't have it. While Tamara's kids have passed the worst and their quarantine period is over, Kyle just came down with it, so it's another round of sickness."

"Why don't we let Sandra go stay at Troy's house? With him in St. Vincent, it'll be ideal. His house is close by and in an upscale gated community, so we shouldn't have any reason to worry about her. I'm sure if we ask him, it won't be a problem."

"No!" Sandra shouted vehemently. "I'd prefer to stay here, or go to a hotel."

Shayne turned quickly, startled by her outburst. When he noticed the glances between Sandra and Carla, he nodded briefly.

"Shayne, you can give Troy a call and find out if it's okay. I'll talk to Sandra. You still have your key for the house here?" Carla asked Shayne.

"Yes, I'm sure he'll say it's fine. I'll call him right now."

He searched around for his cell phone and, finding it, picked it up, dialed and walked out of the room, his voice animated.

"Sandra, you really need to get over this situation. I've always wondered how two mature people who have issues between them never sit down and communicate. I see it in romance novels all the time. The two of you need to talk or you'll end up hating each other for some silly reason."

Before Sandra could respond, Shayne entered the room. He looked at them sheepishly, realizing something was up.

"I won't ask what going on, since that'll be between

128 *Saved by Her Embrace*

you two ladies. However, I did reach Troy and he said that it's definitely not a problem Sandra staying at his home. I'll take Sandra over there in an hour or so and you take the kids to Dr. Charles. I'll be there as soon as I drop Sandra off."

"Good," Carla said, "I'm glad that's solved. Sandra, you're going to have to pack what you need. I'll let you take one of the cars in case you need to use it. You're still comfortable driving here?"

"Definitely, but I don't plan to do too much driving around. I plan on spending my time just relaxing and reading. I'll take a few of your books, if it's not a problem."

"Sounds good. Seems like I'm going to be spending my time nursing two itching children."

"You'll have your work cut out for you. I'll go upstairs and pack what I'll need for the next week or so. Hopefully, I can be back for my last week. I've enjoyed being with the kids, but you and I really haven't spent much time chatting."

"They have mentioned how much fun they had with you and Troy. Of course, the highlight was their day out with 'Uncle George,' whom they seem to totally enjoy."

Sandra laughed, memories of the day still vivid in her mind. "Yes, George. He's so crazy, and so much fun. By the end of our day out, my side was hurting from all the laughter."

"He does know how to please the kids. Hopefully, one day he'll have his own. He's good with them."

"Carla, are you going to let Sandra go up and pack or

keep her talking?" Shayne said, feigning anger. "Your kids are upstairs calling for you."

"So now that they're sick, they're *my* kids."

"You know the routine. In sickness and health. In this case, it's about the kids, and you are much better with their illnesses than I am."

Sandra stood, glaring at Shayne. "I'll go upstairs and pack. You two can stay down here and have your argument about who takes care of what or whom. See why I don't want to marry anytime soon?"

She exited the room, but not before she heard their laughter and Troy's name floating back at her.

Now she knew that they, she and Troy, seemed to be a source of bedroom conversation for her two friends. She didn't like it one bit.

All Carla's talk and her own speculation didn't mean much when Troy had his own plans for his future.

Upstairs she closed her bag and sat on the bed. Going to Troy's home would be difficult. He wouldn't be there, but she suspected that she would feel his presence, his scent, his image and his magnetism.

There was a knock on the door, and Shayne's voice called. "Sandra, I'm ready as soon as you are. Carla has already left with the kids."

"I'm ready."

"I'll take your bag."

She stood, dragging her bag behind her. She opened the door and Shayne took it. "I just need to get my handbag and I'm right behind you."

The drive to Troy's house took less time than she

expected. She knew that he lived nearby, but she had not expected a mere ten-minute drive.

The guard at the entrance allowed them in when he saw it was Shayne. He informed them that Dr. Whitehall had called to confirm that there would be a female guest staying in his home.

Ten minutes later, after showing her the security system, Shayne was on his way.

Sandra closed and locked the door and turned toward the house. Though Troy wasn't here, she felt as if she had walked into the lion's den.


Troy stood on the balcony of the hotel room where he was staying. Although what he was doing here was important, he missed home.

Immediately, his thoughts went to Sandra. He smiled. She was staying in his house. He wished he were there. He'd love to have her in his bed each night.

There he was again, doing the on-again, off-again game with himself. Hadn't he run out of the room the other night because he'd acquired cold feet? Yes, like a coward he'd run from what he was feeling. He knew that he'd hurt her, but at the time he'd only been thinking of himself.

A strained laugh forced its way from him. He was acting like the men in those soap operas or the romance novels all the women he knew loved to read.

It seemed to be the age-old behavior of men. Make love, become scared and run. And he'd definitely run. By the time he returned to Barbados, she'd be gone.

He couldn't even say her name. If he did say it, he

knew that he'd end up thinking about her all night, and definitely get no sleep. As if saying her name aloud would make any difference. Wasn't he thinking about her even now?

He sighed, turned and returned inside.

He glanced at his notes on the table. Work would be the only thing that could take his mind off her. He had surgery to perform tomorrow and one the following day.

He wouldn't be surprised, however, if her scent remained to remind him of his folly.

He sat, picking up the files he had to read. Good. Work and more work equaled no Sandra.

Sunday, Sandra's first day in Troy's house, became an exploration of Troy the man and Troy the doctor. By the end of the day she'd been allowed an insight into what made him the way he was.

Of course, the house may have been decorated by a professional, but it was the small things that touched her in a way she'd not expected.

The interior of the house had been decorated in soft earthy tones, unusual for a man's habitat, but the fixtures and furnishings were definitely masculine. Dark browns were the colors of choice, creating a strong, bold atmosphere that shouted *male.*

His collection of music was strictly from the eighties and nineties, a mixture of R&B, disco and pop music. She'd been surprised to find in his entertainment room a bookshelf overflowing with bestsellers and classics. He had said that he did read, but she'd not realized the extent of his collection. Shakespeare and Dickens shook hands with William Bernhardt, Walter Mosley, Nora Roberts and Brenda Jackson. Another shelf held his medical tomes and journals. All the books appeared well read, and she wondered when he had time to read with his demanding schedule.

When she stepped into his bedroom, his scent assaulted her. The musky, woodsy fragrance of the cologne he wore lingered in the room. The scent titillated her nostrils, stirring an ache inside her.

Next to the bedroom was his office with a computer and stacks and stacks of medical journals. But what surprised her most were the photos on the wall, with letters pinned underneath them. On close examination, she realized that the photos were of his patients, past and present.

Feeling as if she were intruding on his privacy, she detached one of the letters. She couldn't help it.

It was a letter from a little boy.

*Dr. Troy, my mommy told me I could write you. I'm the little boy whose life you saved. I just wanted to thank you and tell you that you're my favorite hero now. I still love Spiderman, but I love you more. I played in a soccer match yesterday and scored the winning goal. I'm back at school and all my friends are happy to see me. I didn't wear a cap as Mommy said I didn't have to. I like my bald head. I think I look like you. Thanks for taking the pain away.*

By the time she reached the third letter, she could read no more; neither could she stem the soft trickle of tears.

She left the room. She'd intruded enough into his life, but she was glad she had. She had a greater appreciation for what he did.

He was a good man…that much she could tell. She'd seen into a part of Troy that he didn't show anyone; one that she'd not expected.

She walked slowly into the TV room feeling pensive. She didn't feel like watching television, so she just sat, and when the room slowly lost its light, she continued to sit in the darkness, her thoughts troubled by what she'd learned.

Had she destroyed what could have been the beginning of her forever by avoiding Troy?

The more she discovered about the man, the heart that beat beneath his chest, the more difficult it was to continue to stifle the feelings he stirred inside her.

What if it were too late to mend what she may have already broken?

Troy walked into the hotel room and slammed the door behind him. He stripped his clothes off and flopped onto the bed.

He couldn't think clearly. He'd arrived in St. Vincent on the first flight from Barbados and two hours later, he'd performed his first surgery. It had gone well and the patient was recovering. Just before he'd left the hospital, his next client, scheduled for surgery the next day, Monday, had died from a massive stroke.

All he could think of was the hopeful, smiling woman. He felt tears sting his eyes. He didn't know why. He felt sad most of the time but he never cried when patients died. He'd been a doctor too long. Inexplicably, the woman's death had affected him deeply.

He picked the phone up. He wanted to hear one of his friends. Shayne.

He dialed the number and Shayne immediately picked up.

"What's wrong?" Shayne asked straight away.

It was the uncanniest thing, but it didn't surprise him. The bond between the three of them—he, Shayne and George—was so strong that there was no need to deny that he wasn't all right.

"One of my patients died today. Just a day before the operation. I should have done it today."

"Troy, you know better than that. Don't blame yourself."

"I know, but I feel responsible. I should have insisted she came over to Barbados to do the surgery."

Shayne didn't reply. He allowed Troy to bare his soul. After half an hour of just chatting, he felt much better.

"Not going to ask about Sandra?" Shayne finally asked.

"I'm sure she's all right. If she wasn't you'd have told me," he responded, trying to sound nonchalant.

"Okay, she is all right. No trace of chicken pox, so she's in the clear. The kids are finally settling down. So what are you going to do now that you don't have the other surgery? Come home?"

"I may just stay put for a few days until Sandra leaves. I don't want to disturb her peace."

"Or you could come back home and keep her company."

When Troy did not respond, Shayne said, "Just kidding. I don't want the two of you to burn down that house you paid so much for."

"Burn it down?" he asked.

"Yeah, with all that heat the two of you generate." Shayne laughed, a loud raucous sound.

"I assure you that that's not going to happen."

"I hear you. I don't know why the two of you don't just admit you love each other and get married."

"Shayne, my brother, I think this is the time I take my leave and get some rest. Talking with you has helped tremendously."

"I'm glad I could help," Shayne replied, a hint of humor still lingering in his tone. "And Troy, I'd suggest that you stop running from your destiny. You and Sandra belong together."

Troy wanted to protest, but disagreeing with Shayne would only open another can of worms.

"Okay, Shayne. Thanks for the advice. I'll call you in a few days."

"As you wish. Seems as if you've made up your mind to stay."

"Yes, I have. Give Carla and the kids my love."

"Will do. Bye."

"Yeah, later," Troy replied.

He put the phone down and switched the light off. All he needed now was to get some sleep. Hopefully, he would wake in the morning feeling a hundred percent better.

Tomorrow, he'd decide what to do.

He fell asleep quickly, but in his dreams saw an image of Sandra naked and lying in his bed…alone.

After two days of doing absolutely nothing but sleeping and reading, the isolation was becoming a bit too much for Sandra. George had promised to drop by tomorrow and she was looking forward to seeing someone other than the woman who came in each day to do a bit of housecleaning and cook lunch. She was grateful she only had to take care of breakfast and a light snack for dinner.

She stepped outside, strolling over to the garden chair outside.

It was late evening, her favorite time of day. The island was absolutely stunning at this time. To the west, the sun was slowly setting. From this part of the island, she could see all the way down to the sea in the distance.

Already the streetlights were flickering on, and the headlights of cars snaked along the highway that led to the north of the island.

She felt at one with nature. She'd grown accustomed to being in the house. At times, she felt close to Troy. Her exploration of the house had left her feelings for him raw and exposed, and she'd done all she could not to think about him.

Each night, she found herself in his bed, his scent offering comfort to her as she hugged his pillow. Each night, she fell asleep like a baby, his voice whispering softly to her.

Each night, she chided herself for the ridiculous way she was behaving, but when she was ready to sleep, the magnetic force of his room found her threading slowly down the corridor until she stood at the entrance. Somehow, being in his bed made her feel closer to him.

Tonight, she stood there for a while, until she finally stepped inside and walked toward the bed. An image of the two of them writhing on the sheets flashed in her mind, belying the restraint she'd been trying to exercise. Her body quaked with her need for him. Exhausted and frustrated, she fell into a tender sleep in which he came to her, placed his arms around her and gently rocked her to sleep.

Each night, the dream she had of him was different. It was never about lovemaking, but something airy and unreal. Mist would swirl around them and they would dance, the skirt of her dress flowing around them. He would be looking down at her, his eyes alive with laughter…and love.

Tonight, he came in black and she wore red, and the strains of a Spanish guitar strummed the chords of a tango, and they danced.

They moved and twisted and gyrated until the dance came to an explosive climax and she stood before him, his lips hovering and his scent strong. In the distance, she heard a noise.

Sandra came suddenly awake. A shadow crossed the threshold of the room and she stayed absolutely still. Was it an intruder? Maybe if she pretended to be asleep, she could come out of this unharmed.

The lights came on, startling her eyes with their

brightness. She screamed despite recognizing the individual.

It was Troy, and he had the nerve to smile.

"Now, now, who's been sleeping in my bed?"

# Chapter 8

"I've been away from home so many times, but this is the first time I've returned to a woman in my bed."

She scrambled off the bed and then went back down, remembering she was wearing a nightshirt that barely covered her legs.

She wrapped the covers around her and sat on the bed.

"I'm sorry. A mouse was in my bedroom. I couldn't sleep in there."

"Mouse? I haven't seen one of those around here in ages," he replied, a broad grin on his face. He *knew* she was lying.

"So, you're going to stay and keep me company tonight?"

"Of course not. I'll go back to my room. The mouse

is probably gone by now." The lie came as easily as a tropical rain.

He laughed. She could tell he didn't believe her. "I'm sure it's gone by now," he said. "Sorry I came back so suddenly."

"It's fine. We'll talk about this tomorrow. I'll check out some hotels."

Before he could respond she exited, the covers draped around her.

There was no way she was staying here with him. She knew exactly what would happen. They'd end up in bed with each other. She was tempted to remain exactly where she was, but staying would be a mistake. She wanted him to respect her, to see her as more than a roll in the hay.

She walked down the corridor slowly, entering her room. She wondered why he was back so early.

How was she going to deal with him? Yes, she would find a hotel or guesthouse and stay there for the next few days. There was a resort her company always used, owned by Taurean Buchanan. Their clients always gushed about the place and she would bet with her contacts she could get it for a reasonable rate for a few days. She'd be sorry to leave here. She liked the house, liked the sense of comfort and security.

She'd been able to relax, and she felt refreshed and revived. When she returned to Atlanta, she'd be back to her old self.

She collapsed on the bed. There was nothing else she could do tonight. One of the things she knew about Troy was that he slept with nothing on, and the thought of him lying naked a few doors away forced images and memories to the surface. She knew he wouldn't come to her room without an invitation, but she knew she wouldn't be doing much sleeping tonight.

Counting sheep or pigs or goats wouldn't help.

Two hours later, her eyes still wide open, she knew that leaving him would be a hard thing to do.

Troy placed the towel in the basket and exited the bathroom, walking naked to the bed.

Lying on his back, he stared up at the ceiling. What had he done? He could have remained in St. Vincent, but the temptation to return home had been too much, especially knowing that the woman he wanted was right here in his home.

When he'd walked into his room and found her lying on his bed, he'd wanted to wake her and make love to her. Even now, his body ached with his arousal and need for her. He realized it was a need that he could no longer kill with a mere kiss. Making love to her didn't work, either. In fact, it only made his desire for her stronger.

He didn't know what to do. When she avoided him, he wanted her. When he made love to her, he wanted her more. There was no compromise, no solution to this gut-wrenching obsession with Sandra.

Was this love? He wasn't sure. He didn't know. He didn't know love. He'd never allowed himself to love before. Ironically, she was the first person he'd felt this way about. The others…had been easy to walk away from.

It was not so with Sandra. Each and every hour of the day, thoughts of her consumed him. He couldn't focus on work. It was all about her, all about the need.

Instinctively, he reached for the phone, but glancing at the clock, he realized it was almost midnight. It was too late to call Shayne. It would disturb his family's sleep.

Each of them was so different, but from their first day in high school, they'd been drawn to each other. He often wondered how they'd become such good friends; Shayne, the introvert, so serious and focused; George, the extrovert, confident and playful; and he, somewhere in between.

On reflection, back then, it had been their love for cricket. Three totally different individuals, but put a cricket ball or bat in their hands and they'd play the game all day.

But so much had changed. They rarely went to matches anymore, rarely spent time together. But they still loved each other with a power that only a man could understand. He'd give his life for each of his friends.

Change was good, they said, but there was a part of him that hated change. He liked things as they were. Change often brought out the negative…and loneliness.

He was lonely. He hated to admit it, but he was lonely.

Though he loved his godchildren, there were times he hated to go over to the Knight Plantation. It only made him realize what was missing from his life—a wife and children. But marriage would come later.

There were still so many things he wanted to achieve in his career; among them, to head the neurosurgery unit at the hospital.

His dreams, his aspirations, were all connected to his work, but at night, when he lay in bed as he did now, he felt so alone. His body ached with his loneliness, a dull throbbing ache that did nothing to ease his current state of mind.

He had a great million-dollar home, the ideal job and the best of friends, but he was lonely.

He tried to purge the thought from his mind, but an hour later, he still stared at the ceiling.

He was still alone.

The next morning, Sandra woke, her body tired from the lack of sleep. She had stayed awake until the early hours of the morning.

She felt grumpy and miserable. She would take a shower and go downstairs to chat with Troy before he left for work. She didn't want to leave without thanking him for letting her stay.

She quickly showered and donned the most con-servative thing she could find. She didn't want him getting the wrong idea. However, she did place a bit of gloss on her lips, something she didn't normally do, and a quick glance in the mirror and she was good to go.

Downstairs, she headed immediately for the kitchen. He wasn't there, and she wondered if she should have knocked on his bedroom door to see if he was awake.

In the kitchen, she glanced out the window to the garage and noticed his car was still parked.

She made breakfast for the two of them; it was the least she could do to show her appreciation. Later, she'd call the resort, make alternate arrangements and leave before he returned from work. Though things were changing between them, staying here would lead to the inevitable. They'd end up in bed, and while she still yearned for him, she didn't want the start of her changed relationship with him to be only about sex.

Ten minutes later, fluffy omelets made and coffee percolating, she was ready to eat. She hoped he'd come down soon.

As if on cue, he entered the kitchen.

"Something smells good. I could eat a horse, so I'm hoping I'm included in that savory feast." He sounded chirpy. She'd never seen him so happy.

"I made enough for two. I just need to toast the bread. Light or dark?" she asked, trying to keep her eyes off him. How did a man look so sexy so early in the morning?

"It really doesn't matter. I'll eat anything. I'm just hungry." He walked over to one of the stools at the counter and sat.

"Didn't realize you had such a hearty appetite," she said, placing several slices of bread into the toaster.

"There's a lot you don't know about me, and a lot I don't know about you."

She didn't respond, but what he'd said was true. They didn't know much about each other beyond the bed.

"Maybe we could use this time to get to know each other," he continued.

"I was planning on checking into a resort. I'm not sure if it's a good idea for me to stay around."

"While it may not seem the best thing for you," he said, "I can make it easy. I spend most of my time at the hospital so if it's really a question of not wanting to be around me, I can make it possible. I usually leave for work early in the morning and get home late at night. You won't even have to see me. The choice is really yours, but I don't see the need for you to spend money at a hotel. I know Shayne and Carla would prefer you to be close."

"I'll think about it and let you know my answer when you come home."

"If you really want to avoid me, just leave a note on the table here and I'll see it," he said. She could hear the sarcasm in his voice. "I think it's time I head out for work. Thanks for the breakfast."

"You haven't eaten it," she said.

"I'm really not hungry," he replied. Nodding abruptly, he turned and left.

She'd hurt his feelings. She'd thought he'd be happy that she would go.

For a long time, she sat quietly, wondering what to do. Maybe he was right. She could stay at the house. She knew he was a workaholic, so she really didn't need to see him much. She'd show her appreciation by making breakfast for him each morning and then he'd be off to work. No hassle, no unnecessary contact. By the time he came in at night, she'd make sure she was in bed.

As she was drying the final dish, the phone began to ring.

She glanced at the cordless phone nearby. It was Carla's morning call. She looked forward to them. Being by herself could be claustrophobic at times.

"Hi, Carla."

"Hi, sweetheart. And how are you this morning? I hope you slept well." She could not help but hear the humor in Carla's voice.

"So I'm the only one who didn't know that Troy was coming home."

"Sandra, I just found out. Troy just called Shayne on his way to work. We didn't know."

"How are the kids doing?" she asked.

"Darius is more than frustrated. He's tired of being indoors. I'm allowing them to go outside and play today, so he should be a lot less irritable. Lynn-Marie is a trouper and takes everything in stride. She just wants to be in Mommy or Daddy's arms and she's fine. She realized the best thing to do is sleep. The lotion that the doctor gave us has helped a lot. It's only their incubation period I have to deal with now, but at least, since Tamara's kids had it, they can come over."

"I don't envy you."

"Sandra, I know how you feel about kids. You'll make a good mother. There is no one I felt safer leaving my kids with when we went cruising. I know they missed us when we were on the cruise, but having a doting godmother helps. They had fun with you and Troy."

There was silence, as the name hovered in the air.

"So what are you going to do?" Carla asked.

"I was thinking about going to stay at the resort owned by Taurean Buchanan. It's got itself a great reputation for quality and class. And it's definitely reasonable."

"Why would you have to do that? Troy won't have a problem with your staying there." She paused for a bit. "Unless you're worried about what *can* happen."

"What can happen?" she answered innocently.

"Come off it, Sandra. You know exactly what I mean. I can't get a handle on what the two of you are doing. And I don't mean to offend, but the two of you need to grow up and stop playing kids' games. In fact, I'm not even sure if the two of you are ready for a relationship. At least, with each other."

Well, that was telling it like it is. Sandra wasn't sure how to respond.

"Can we not talk about Troy right now? I'll think about what you said."

"Good, you'll let me know what you intend to do. You still have the car, so you can drive yourself to the resort if you want. Just call me for directions."

"Thanks, Carla. I'll talk to you later."

Sandra put the phone down. What Carla had said hurt, but she could not deny it. That's the kind of friend Carla was. She told it as it was.

She walked out of the kitchen, making sure that she left the room as tidy as she'd found it. One thing she realized was that Troy liked his surroundings neat and clean. She moved slowly, still unsure of what to do. By the time she reached her room, she'd weighed the pros and cons, and the pros far outweighed the cons. In fact, she could think of only one reason why she would have to leave, and it was because she didn't want to end up in bed with him.

Not that she didn't long for him to make love to her, but because she knew that the contact would be just that, physical contact.

But wasn't that how most relationships began?

Troy tried to focus on the words of the chief of staff, but he couldn't. He was still annoyed by what had happened that morning.

"Troy?" He turned to Dr. Craig. "I'd suggest we continue this meeting later. Something's bothering you?"

He wasn't sure how to respond, but he chose his words carefully. Dr. Craig was a taskmaster and expected nothing less than perfection from his subordinates, especially those vying to take over his job.

"You've been distracted for the past three weeks. Even today you seem more distracted. I thought going to St. Vincent would have taken care of whatever you were dealing with. I can't have one of my head surgeons in this state."

Troy stared at him steadily, knowing that what he'd said was true, but there was something annoying about what was happening here.

He'd given most of his life to this hospital. Almost fifteen years since leaving medical school in Jamaica and then returning to Barbados to be an intern. He'd worked hard and long, long hours and this one time, when he was distracted, he got the third degree. It took all of his willpower not to give the man a piece of his mind and walk away.

Instead, he smiled sweetly and then said, "I assure you, I'm fine, Dr. Craig, but I think it's best I leave and head on home. I've just spent six hours in surgery and I'm tired. Sorry if that doesn't fit into your prerequisites for my being a good surgeon, but to be honest, right now I really don't care. If my record and hard work don't mean anything much, then maybe I'm not in the right place."

He stood, indifference evident in his stance.

"And I wish you a good night, sir. Pass on my greetings to your lovely wife."

He walked out without looking back, knowing if he did he would probably start laughing. Everyone in the hospital knew that Dr. Craig's wife was sleeping with one of the young doctors at the hospital. One day, Dr. Craig would find out. He only hoped that he was around when the arrogant SOB found out.

As he walked down the corridor, he found himself whistling softly. Fortunately, his office was not in the section of the hospital where the wards were, but he suspected that if anyone heard him, he'd be reprimanded.

He pulled his cell phone out and called George.

"What are you doing this evening, buddy?"

"Nothing," George replied. "You want to go Bert's and get something to eat?"

"No problem. I'm actually getting ready to leave the hospital, and I'm starving."

"Good, I'll meet you there in half an hour."

"I'll be there."

When he walked into the bar an hour later, he wasn't surprised that George wasn't there. George was never on time for social gatherings. Not that he could complain, he didn't do much better with time; the unpredictability of his job was his excuse. Just as he was leaving the hospital, he'd been called to see one of his patients.

He headed immediately for the bar. He wanted a drink. He drank only socially, but even then limited himself to one or two.

Tonight, he felt like drinking until he could fall asleep and forget the woman in the bedroom down the hall.

"So what you having tonight?" Herbert, the bartender, asked. "Haven't seen you in here for a while. George complains that you've been working too much."

He shrugged, climbing onto one of the stools. "I can't argue with that, Herb. I have been working a lot."

"I know, man, but you still have to get out sometimes and enjoy life. Hang with the guys. Haven't seen your other partner lately, either. He must be enjoying the married life. I remember the days when you'd all be in here every weekend."

"Yeah, those days are over."

"Wonder which of you will be the next to go?"

"Next to go?"

"I mean get married. And from the look on your face, it must be some beauty that has you looking so troubled."

"I look troubled?"

"You must remember, Dr. Whitehall, that I've been working here since you boys turned seventeen and tried to sneak in here. I made you wait until you were legal. So I've grown to know each of you. I *know* when you have a woman on your mind. I see it every night when customers come in here with woman problems. But you're a good man, so I'm sure that whatever you're dealing with will work itself out. She'll melt at that smile and she'll be all yours." He laughed, a loud, happy sound. "Unless you're the one giving trouble. Must be what George says. You're always working."

"Well, it's my hard work that saves people's lives and keeps my mind focused on reality."

"I believe you're trying to convince yourself of that. I hope that *work* keeps you *warm* at night. Well, George is heading over here. I'll get him his drink."

Troy turned in the direction of the entrance and watched his best friend swagger toward him.

In high school George had been an amateur body builder, and back then he'd been really massive. In recent years, he'd modified his training program and he'd given up the excessive muscles for a leaner look, but his well-toned body was still a wide expanse of broad shoulders and bulging arms and legs.

Troy was one of the few who knew that under all

the outward confidence hid a man who still dealt with his uneasiness about his height. Only his close friends knew that he hated his height.

George stopped before him and hoisted himself onto the empty stool next to him.

"Half an hour, you said," Troy scolded.

"I did? I was sure I said an hour," George responded, laughter on his face.

"Sure, George you are always late."

"I'm sorry. I was distracted a bit at work," he said with a shy grin.

"Donna White?"

"The one and only. Had to pry her off me. I was about to leave when she walked into my office. Wanted us to do it right then and there. Unfortunately, since I had plans on meeting you, I had to turn down the offer. But she did insist that I—"

"Spare me the sordid details," Troy interrupted. "I'm well aware of what she's capable of doing."

Herbert interrupted them briefly to place George's drink on the bar.

"Thanks, Herb."

"You want a waitress to take you to your table?" Herbert asked.

"Yeah, I'm hungry," George replied. "You ready to eat, Troy?"

"Definitely," Troy replied.

Nodding at Herbert, they followed the waitress he'd called.

After ordering their usual grilled fish, French fries

and lots of pepper sauce and ketchup, they sat quietly, watching a rerun of one of last season's NBA matches.

"So what's going on, Troy?" George eventually asked. "Why are you back in Barbados already?"

"The second patient I had to operate on died. The other operation was postponed."

"Sorry to hear about that."

"She should have had that surgery done months ago."

"You did all that you could."

"I suppose so. The hospital was waiting for the insurance company to approve the surgery."

"Well, you know my opinion on insurance companies. I think they are the scum of the earth," George said, the lawyer in him coming to the fore.

"I don't know if I'd go that far, since most of my patients wouldn't be able to afford the surgeries without them, but it's the time the paperwork takes that really pisses me off," Troy said, his calm tone suppressing his anger.

"If you say so," George replied.

"And what about your upcoming case? You're ready to face the trial of your life?"

"Of course I'm ready."

Troy looked at his friend closely.

"Do I detect a note of reservation?"

George didn't answer.

"I'm listening."

"Guess who's trying the case?" George asked, piquing Troy's curiosity.

"Who? I'm intrigued," Troy asked

George didn't reply.

"No, not her?" Troy said in disbelief.

"Yes, her." George mumbled, shrugging his shoulders.

"Oh, my God. I'd love to be in that courtroom. The sparks are going to fly and combust." Troy chuckled.

"But she hates me."

"The best thing she has ever done. I hope she whups your ass in court."

"And you're supposed to be my best friend."

"Rachel's my friend, too. And the way you treated her left so much to be desired."

"How can you say that?" George grunted. "You know how I felt about her."

"Because you weren't man enough to admit you loved her and allowed her to marry that man almost twice her age."

"She said she wanted stability. I couldn't offer her that."

"You should have. You didn't want to. Damn hang-up about the fact that she's taller than you."

"You're the last person who should be talking about hang-ups. You have the hots for Miss Atlanta and you're running scared. You're no different from me," George retorted.

"From you? You can't compare my relationship with Sandra to yours and Rachel's. The girl was in love with you. Everyone knew it. Had been in love with you since both of you were in high school. You two could be married with at least three kids by now."

He saw George's mock shudder and laughed. "You make a sport of all this. I suspect that having Rachel around is only going to make you long to have her. I'll be watching what's going on with interest."

"So you plan on wasting your time watching me when you should be taking care of your own situation," George replied.

"Good, the food is here," Troy said, ignoring George's comment. "Change the conversation or I'll make you shut up with all the nonsense you're saying."

"It doesn't matter to me one way or the other. I'll be the first and last one laughing," George responded.

Troy's laughter echoed through the room. He smiled. He knew beyond a shadow of doubt that George would be the first to bite the dust.

It certainly wouldn't be him!

# Chapter 9

When Troy entered the house several hours later, it was with the hope that Sandra was fast asleep. From all indications in the darkened house, she was in bed.

He sighed in relief. He didn't want to see her tonight. In the mood he was in, the slight adrenaline that came from drinking a glass of wine made him vulnerable.

He climbed the stairs wondering if she'd stayed awake, wondering where he was, but discarded the thought.

The idea of Sandra being awake waiting for him was ludicrous. She was probably hoping he'd return to St. Vincent, or she was already packed to leave. At least she hadn't left for the resort. Maybe she planned on staying.

At the top of the stairs, he turned right, heading to

his room. When he passed hers, he stopped. He could hear nothing. Not even a sliver of light peeped under the door. She was definitely asleep.

He quickly moved along and entered his bedroom, stripped, dropped his clothes in the basket and headed straight for the shower.

Twenty minutes later, he stepped out of the shower, his body soothed by the cool water on his heated, weary body.

He dried quickly, put on a pair of long sleep pants and headed back downstairs. A cup of tea before he went to sleep would let him rest comfortably, he hoped.

When he entered the kitchen this time, it was not empty. Sandra, at the counter, turned at the sound of his footsteps. The look of dread on her face only confirmed what he'd been thinking.

"Good night," she said politely, her voice strained and expressionless.

"And good night to you, too," he replied. "I promise I won't stay long. Just want to get a cup of tea and I'm off to sleep."

"You're being here doesn't bother me," she responded. "You can stay as long as you want. It's your house."

"We did make a deal, didn't we? I know you'd prefer not to see me."

"As I said, it really doesn't matter."

"If I didn't know you, I'd think you're annoyed with me for coming in late."

"Me, annoyed? I assure you, that is not it. Why

would I be annoyed that you're late? I'd prefer if I didn't have to see you."

She stopped, realizing what she'd said.

"Now you see what I mean. In one breath you're telling me that having me around doesn't bother you and in the next, you're telling me you don't want to see me. Which is it? I think the lady protests too much."

"That has always been the problem with you. You're so arrogant and conceited. You think that every woman wants you."

"Every woman. I'm not interested in every woman, Sandra. This is about you and me. I know you want me."

She stood quickly, stepped forward and slapped him across the face.

He turned to face her again. His face hurt a bit, but he refused to allow her to see his discomfort.

"So what do you want me to do? I have two choices. I kiss you or I slap you back. Since I'm not one to raise my hands to a lady, I'm going to have to kiss you."

She raised her hand again, but in one smooth movement, he grabbed it and pulled her against him.

She struggled to get away, but he pulled her even closer, restricting her movements.

He lowered his mouth toward hers, his breath a whisper.

"I love a feisty woman."

She opened her mouth to respond but immediately realized her mistake.

His lips covered hers, his mouth firm, coaxing her

into surrendering. For a while she resisted, but when she surrendered, she did it with a sigh of resignation.

If he were not kissing her, he knew he'd be smiling. He felt as if he'd won a long battle and that out of this kiss, this touching of lips, this compromise, they'd finally accepted what they had long failed to acknowledge—that they wanted each other, not for the physical gratification they took for granted, but for that rare connection of heart and soul.

They continued to kiss, their lips touching, hearts beating against each other's.

"I want to make love to you," he finally said, the need for her evident in the huskiness of his voice.

She stared at him for a long time, the uncertainty plain on her face. He couldn't blame her for her caution. He'd given her nothing but indifference and selfishness.

"What is it going to be, Troy? Another round of free sex for us and then we move on until the next time we decide we want each other again?"

He felt his face warm, embarrassed by what she'd said, ashamed that she was right, but he wanted things to be different. He wanted more, much more.

"I won't lie. I want you. In fact, I need you. I don't know what all this means, but I'm tired of this on-again, off-again relationship we have. I want more, but I don't know what more I have to offer."

She paused for a moment. He could tell that she was thinking, contemplating what he'd said. Her face registered her acceptance.

"Maybe we should agree to give us a chance," she

eventually said. "That may be the problem. We've never given *us* a chance."

"That's true. Maybe this is the time for us to take a chance on each other," he responded.

"Then we can talk about the logistics later. Right now I need you to make love to me," she admitted without hesitation.

He could not help but stare at her. She'd somehow transformed once again into this confident, sexy individual who knew what she wanted.

He couldn't complain. The hunger he felt was a hunger for her, and nothing else could ease the ache he felt deep down inside.

In the bedroom, he planted her feet on the ground and groaned in relief. He'd lifted her up and walked with her up the stairs, an action he knew he'd regret tomorrow. He needed to remember he was no longer in his twenties.

Pride gave him the strength to take her to the top, but he sighed with relief when he reached the landing. In the movies, didn't the heroes make this seem so easy and romantic?

They stood facing each other, their bodies barely touching as they both hesitated, still unsure of the step they were about to take.

Sandra made the first move. She reached for him, her palms lying flat against his chest. She touched him gently, allowing her fingers to trail along his chest until they played with his nipples, pinching and squeezing them between her fingers.

He stood still, the only evidence of his reaction the stiffening of his body.

She leaned forward, placing her lips against his chest until her mouth found a firm, hard nipple. She teased the other one between her fingers, pleased when he moaned softly.

Her hands and fingers caressed him, trailing downward until they reached the waistband of his pants and slowly worked them down.

His penis stood hard and erect, and Sandra knew immediately she wanted him buried inside her.

Her hands gripped him, feeling the instant jerk of response. She trailed her hand along its length, loving the firm, velvety feel. She'd never been fascinated by a penis before, but there was something about his that made her whole body hot and wet. She stroked him gently.

A deep, low groan echoed his pleasure, and she felt him tremble while his thick length throbbed hot in her hands.

She pushed him backward onto the bed. She loved him in that position, vulnerable and exposed, his penis standing straight up, proud and magnificent. She felt strong and in control.

She lay on top of him, careful not to hurt him with her weight, but he placed his arms around her, drawing her closer, his lips finding hers again.

The kiss was one of desperation, as if their mouths had not touched in ages.

She returned the kiss, loving the feel of his body against hers. Their tongues entwined, teasing each other. Heat coursed through her until she felt as if her body would combust unless he did something about it.

"Take your clothes off," he said.

She obliged, slipping out of the nightshirt she wore as quickly as she could. A sudden burst of air from the air-conditioning unit gave her a brief moment of relief from the heat within.

When she lay on top of him, he flipped her over, his hard body against her, intensifying her arousal. His penis, hard and erect, pressed against her stomach. He moved his hips slightly, allowing his hardened length to slide up and down. There was something so powerfully erotic about his movement that she could feel the moisture of her readiness.

His mouth captured one of her nipples, tugging on it with his teeth. A flash of heat surged through her, her body feeling hot and wet at the same time.

He moved to the other breast, his mouth working its magic again, so that the heat inside her made its way downward until the core of her womanhood felt empty, longing to be filled.

His mouth moved downward until it paused over that special mound. He touched her gently, his tongue slipping between the tender folds. His tongue was hot yet felt slippery and wet inside, until she felt a flicker against the sensitive nub. His tongue teased and tugged, causing her body to buck like a wild horse. The muscles of her body tensed and relaxed with each of his ministrations, and inside the heat intensified.

When her release came, she grabbed his hair, her

cries of ecstasy filling the room. Her body shivered uncontrollably until she felt that it would never stop.

Troy raised his head, shifting until he was above her, his arms spanning her body.

He moved her legs apart, giving himself entry, and then he guided the full length of his penis inside her. He moved his pelvis backward and then moved firmly forward. She gasped with the power of his entry. Her vagina grasped him tightly, pulsating around him. She could feel the fullness of his length inside her, the snakelike veins. She widened her legs, curling them around his waist, allowing his manhood to slide farther in until she could feel its head lodged against her sweet spot.

And then he started to love her with a firm backward and forward movement that caused her to groan loudly.

Troy changed his movement and stroked her quickly, grinding his hips from left to right, touching every sensitive spot within her. Her groan of pleasure only served to stoke the fire burning inside him.

Beneath him, Sandra's body started its own movement, meeting him halfway.

He shifted her body, letting her lie partially on her side, and then he continued his stroking. The position allowed him deeper penetration, until he could feel every soft inch of her sweetness. With each stroke she cried out, begging him not to stop, urging him to stroke harder and harder.

And he worked his magic. He took her to the edge and then, when he felt her body tense with release, he pulled her back, starting the journey all over again.

When he felt he could take it no more, he increased his speed, moving his body against hers with a force that she matched with her own movement. He knew it. She knew it. The ending was near. The sweet powerful release was coming. He could feel it in every nerve of his body.

And then it happened. His body stiffened and his stroking became awkward and jerky. But he continued to stroke her. His body tensed and his muscles tightened, and he felt the length of his manhood expand and contract. When he groaned out loud, it was the cry of a warrior, a cry that came from deep inside his gut.

He felt the surge of energy inside him, and the powerful release of his seed rendered him helpless as spasm after spasm racked his body. Under him, Sandra shuddered and groaned and tensed against him. With one final cry, he collapsed against her. She pulled him closer as her own orgasm followed. Her body shook and convulsed with the power of her release.

Finally, their breathing calmed, and she held on to him as if she'd never let go.

He kissed her gently on her lips and the last word he heard before he fell asleep was *incredible*.

During the night, Troy woke, immediately aware of the delicious presence against him. His manhood hardened. He wanted her again and knew that before morning he'd have her again.

Beside him, she stirred.

He jumped from the bed. He needed to take a shower. He wished she'd wake, but she slept like a baby.

In the shower, he turned the water on, adjusting the water to cool. His body felt heated, and hopefully the coolness would calm him.

He heard the door open and the curtain pulled aside.

She smiled shyly and he smiled in return. She stepped inside and he pulled her to him, kissing her, wanting to reassure her that this was not like the past.

She relaxed and melted against him, her softness pressing into him. He loved that part of her. She loved to cuddle and press herself against him as if she wanted them to become one body.

He kissed her tenderly on the nose, her eyes, her lips. His lips moved downward, capturing one turgid nipple between his teeth.

She groaned with desire. He stopped, lifting his head, and looked closely at her.

"Any regrets?" he finally asked.

"Now? No," she replied. "For now, just let's take every day as it comes."

He nodded and lowered his head to take her lips with his. At the same time, he parted her legs with his and guided his penis inside her. The sensation that spread through his body caused him to moan with pleasure.

Slowly, firmly, he stroked her, his only thought that he'd found a place to belong.

Troy woke in the early hours of the morning. He opened his eyes to the usual silence that greeted him. He sighed. Another day of hard work and nothingness… and then it all came back to him. The incredible night he'd had with Sandra.

He glanced at the empty spot next to him and realized she was gone. A moment of trepidation filled him and then he realized she must still be here.

He'd never experienced that emotion before, but he felt a strong shame at the times he'd done it to his women friends.

He'd always left without a thought of how his friends felt when they woke up and found him gone. A part of him had enjoyed the fact that he'd left them so drained from his lovemaking they didn't realize he had left.

He turned over on his back, his body feeling weary and satiated. He wanted to get up, but he wasn't sure he could. They'd made love all night long. Each time he woke during the night, he'd wanted her. Each time he'd drawn her to him and they'd explored each other's bodies in a way they'd never done before.

He still wasn't sure what this was all leading to, but he knew he wanted to give them a chance to see what was possible.

There was a part of him that was afraid. He'd dreamed so often of following in his father's footsteps, and he knew that to develop a relationship that went beyond his usual ones could lead to trouble.

He'd observed his mother and father's marriage for years and had always thought she was happy. Now he wondered if she'd given up a part of herself devoting her life to his father and to him. He needed to talk to her about this. A part of him felt that he'd been selfish, but maybe that had been the choice she made because she loved him.

On reflection, he realized that his father had not been the perfect father. His father had never shown an interest in anything he did—until he'd decided to be a doctor. Then his father had always been there for him. At that time, he'd adored his father. His father had always been there to encourage him to be the best. And he'd been the best. At no time in his school life had he ever received a grade below an A.

He had been the topic of his father's conversation at functions. But something stuck in his mind. All the things he'd loved doing had come second to his father's dreams for him. His cricketing days had come to an end and he'd drifted slowly away from his best friends for a time.

It was only when he'd graduated that he'd renewed his friendship with them, but the partying and cricket matches had come to an end.

He paused his thoughts. He didn't want to think about his father. He wanted to see Sandra. He took a quick shower and in no time was walking into the kitchen.

Disappointment filled him when she wasn't there. Where was she?

He noticed a note on the table and picked it up.

*You were fast asleep. Tamara and I are going into Bridgetown. I'll be back in the afternoon.*

Again a wave of disappointment washed over him. He missed her. He wanted to see her. Even now, thoughts of their night together flashed before him.

He felt his manhood harden. He was beginning to act like a teenager, but he didn't care. The thought of making love to her again was too appealing. It was probably a good thing she wasn't here.

He would make and eat breakfast, and then go to the hospital for a short while to see the patient he'd operated on the day before. Maybe having something to focus on would help him not to think about her.

The phone rang and he picked it up, glancing at the caller ID at the same time.

"Hello, Dad."

"I heard from Dr. Craig that you were back from St. Vincent."

"Yes, I returned two days ago. I didn't stay the full week as I'd planned. One of my patients died before the surgery."

"I hear that congratulations are in order. Your surgery yesterday seems to have been a success. All of the senior staff are impressed. I'm proud of you, son."

"Thanks, Dad. I didn't realize I was impressing the senior staff."

"Oh, you are, son. You certainly have the tongues wagging. This is a short call. I'm taking your mother out to lunch."

"That's great, Dad. To the Brown Sugar Restaurant, right?"

"You know that's her favorite place. Hold on. She wants to say hi. See you later, son."

"Morning, sweetheart." His mother's voice came over the line.

"How are you, Mom?"

"I'm fine. Of course, I'm sure your dad told you he's

taking me out to lunch. I'm sorry we didn't invite you to join us."

"It's fine, Mom. We'll do something together in a few days. I have to go into the hospital to check on a patient."

"You're going into work on your off day? You need to get some rest. Working yourself to death like your dad?"

"I'm fine, Mom. I'll get some rest today."

"I spoke to Shayne recently. He told me that lovely girl, Carla's friend, is here. What's her name now? Yes, Sandra. She's so nice."

*Damn, he could tell where this conversation was going.* "Yes, Mom, I know. She's here," he replied.

"Shayne did say she's staying at your house until the kids are out of quarantine. I'm not sure that's proper, but under the circumstances, I'll expect you to treat her like a lady. I think she's a lovely girl and would make some lucky man a wonderful wife."

He wasn't sure how he was expected to respond, but he knew exactly what his mother was hinting at. His mother believed that he should have been married years ago.

"She'd make you a good wife. I know she likes you. I see how she looks at you."

"Okay, Mom. You're imagining things."

"Is she there? I'd love to say hi to her."

"Sorry, she's not here. She left a note that she was going into Bridgetown with Tamara."

"Oh, you must bring her over for dinner before she leaves, so we girls can chat."

"I'll do that. I have to leave to go to the hospital. I want to be back home soon."

"Good, I don't want you spending your whole day off there," she commented.

"I won't, Mom," he said compliantly.

"Promise me?" she replied emphatically.

"Yes, promise you. Love you."

With that he put the phone down. His conversation with his mother had got him thinking. Did everyone know how he felt about Sandra? He'd tried his hardest to hide how he felt, tried to make sure that when she was in close proximity he didn't stare at her too long, though he knew that over the years his gaze had lingered.

On reflection, he realized that over the years, he'd inquired about her.

He paused. He needed to stop thinking about her.

Troy planned his day out in his mind while he prepared one of his special omelets. He'd go to the hospital, return home and watch a cricket match he wanted to catch on television, and then he would take Sandra out to dinner. Maybe they'd stop by his mother's home. He already knew how his mother would react, but maybe that would stop her matchmaking.

After a breakfast of his favorite omelet, a glass of cranberry juice and he was ready to start his day.

Good, no Sandra Walters to confuse his mind. For a few hours he didn't have to deal with the emotional state of mind he seemed to be in every day since Sandra came to the island.

A few minutes later, he closed the door and headed for the hospital. It was there he felt safe, where he could forget about all the issues and things tossing around in his mind.

# Chapter 10

Sandra had not planned on going into the city, but when Tamara had called and asked her to go shopping with her, she'd agreed willingly. Saturday in Bridgetown was an event not to be missed.

Not that she'd been running away from what had happened the night before, but she needed to get away from Troy. To say that the night had been a passionate one would have been to limit what had happened between them.

And that's what scared her. She knew they'd talked about giving the relationship a chance, to see where things would go, but the magnitude of her epiphany in the midst of their lovemaking had startled her.

She was in love with Troy Whitehall. The realization, now she admitted it, that she'd loved him for a long time made her feel vulnerable and fragile, but she was by no means a fragile individual.

*Strong, confident, independent* and *outspoken* were words others would use to describe her character, but today she didn't feel like any of those words.

Last night, Troy had taken her to a place she'd never been before. She'd never known such passion and fulfillment, and the fact that she knew he'd been affected in the same way had scared her.

But a part of her wanted to wake up each morning, as she had done this morning, and find him sleeping next to her.

When she'd stepped out of bed, she'd sat in a chair next to the bed and stared at him until he'd started to slowly stir.

She'd raced downstairs to prepare breakfast, and when her cell phone had gone off she'd answered, immediately accepting when Tamara had asked her to join her.

She glanced up when Tamara reappeared.

"Sorry I took so long. You're ready to order?"

"I've glanced at the menu and everything looks so good. What's the best thing here?" she asked, putting the menu down.

"Oh, everything is good, but today I'm getting a large bowl of cou-cou with lots of gravy, and fried plantains."

At the expression on Sandra's face, she added, "I'm surprised you haven't had it before. It's our national dish, make of okras and cornmeal. Just trust me. You're going to ask me to bring you back here another time just to taste this wonderful dish."

"Well, I put myself totally in your hands," Sandra consented.

Tamara called the waitress over, gave the order and then turned back to Sandra.

"So how are you enjoying your stay?"

"It's been good."

"Only good? You and Troy? I would have thought that the sparks would be flying."

Sandra did not respond. *Did everyone know about them?*

"Now you've got me curious, and that blush on your face tells a million tales. I promise I won't tell."

"If I tell you, Carla is going to be so angry. I always tell her first."

"Since she is indisposed and she is my sister-in-law, I am sure she won't mind that I'm willing to lend an ear and be her substitute."

Sandra laughed.

"And I know that you and Troy have the hots for each other," Tamara continued. "And you are staying at his house. That house must be shaking each night."

At Sandra's blush, she continued, "So it's true. It's about time. I keep wondering when the two of you are going to realize that you want each other and do something about it."

"It's not the first time, you know," Sandra said.

"Not the first time? You mean you've tasted that gorgeous man already? Girlfriend, I didn't even realize that the two of you did the dirty already. I'm so proud of you. So how is he?"

"Tamara!" Sandra exclaimed.

"Girlfriend, I may look like the quiet type, but I love me some good sex and Kyle knows how to use his mojo. So I'm going to ask again. How is he?"

Sandra really wasn't sure what to say, but eventually she lowered her inhibitions. Tamara listened with rapt interest.

"Oh, my God. This is so, so…hot. I can't believe that Troy has such passion in his body. I know he has passion for his work. He does everything with an intensity. It must be you. God made you for him, so that's why you have that impact on him."

Sandra laughed in response. She felt good. They ate and chatted.

"You ready to continue our shopping?" Tamara asked. "There is the loveliest pair of shoes in Mademoiselle, just next door. Kyle and I have a dinner coming up. His latest book has made the bestseller list and his editor is on the island on a working holiday. She gets to meet with one of her best clients and still enjoy the beach and lots of sunshine. You *have* been to be beach since you were here?"

"Several times," Sandra replied. "I wish I could go every day, but most days I just feel like reading and relaxing."

"And making love. You can't forget that."

"Right now, I'd prefer to forget."

"Why? Because it brings images you'd prefer to forget?"

"No, because it brings images I can't seem to forget. Images that make my body ache to have him again."

Tamara stared at her silently. When she finally spoke, it was with the voice of a woman happily married.

"I have no doubt that you and Troy are going to become lovers in the true sense of the word. There is too much going on between the two of you."

"Maybe, maybe not. Maybe that's the only way to save him from a life that's only work."

"Good. I am sure you don't want him ending up like your father or his father. If there is anyone who can make him see reason, it is you. I'm rooting for you."

Sandra did not respond. Things were happening a bit too quickly for her.

She watched Tamara pay the waitress and beckon for her to follow.

At least for the next few hours she'd be able to forget Troy. There was nothing she enjoyed more than a few hours of shopping with her good friend.

The next day, Sandra received the all clear from Carla. She'd be able to return to the Knight Plantation tomorrow. She realized immediately that she didn't want to leave. She wondered if Troy would ask her to stay. Last night, he'd come to her bed in the middle of the night and she'd melted in his arms, her reservations about their relationship no longer an issue. She knew now that what existed between the two of them was more than what it had been. The night of making love and talking had changed things. She wanted more, but what was more? She wasn't sure.

The thought of a serious commitment still scared her, but she was willing to take the risk to see what would happen.

In the middle of the night, after making love, Troy had given in to her craving for ice cream and gone downstairs, returning with two large bowlfuls of rum-and-raisin ice cream.

They'd laughed and talked about nothing and about everything. No conversation was off-limits. Sandra discovered that they had lots of things in common. They both loved the old classic movies. Actors like Humphrey Bogart, Claudette Colbert, Sidney Poitier and John Wayne were high on their list of favorites.

They also enjoyed the same kind of music. The jazz greats, Louis Armstrong, Billie Holliday, Miles Davis and Benny Goodman were frequently in their home entertainment centers.

In the morning he'd awakened her, planted a soft kiss on her cheek and said he was off to work.

She'd smiled and fallen right back to sleep, until two hours later, when the phone had rung, and Carla had given her the news.

A few days ago she'd have called the news good; now she dreaded leaving.

During the day, she helped the housekeeper with some cleaning, wanting to keep herself occupied.

Now, as the sun slipped below the horizon, she sat on a chair on the patio and drifted off to sleep.

She woke suddenly; someone was shaking her.

"You plan on sleeping there all evening?"

*What a great way to wake up,* she thought.

Troy bent to kiss her lightly on the lips.

"How'd you like to go out to dinner?" he asked.

She hesitated, making sure she had purchased something appropriate to wear. Yes, the red dress would be perfect!

"That's fine."

"Good, I made reservations at a restaurant for seven o'clock, so get on up and do what you ladies do to make yourself beautiful."

"So I'm not beautiful naturally?" she responded, trying to feign hurt.

"Of course. I think you're the most beautiful woman I know. Well, after Halle Berry."

She laughed. "Okay, I can accept that."

She stood. "As you suggested, I'll go upstairs and do whatever it takes to make me more beautiful. I bought the cutest little number yesterday when I went shopping with Tamara."

"My God, no wonder you were fast asleep. I've heard all about Tamara and her shopping. Twenty-four hours and you're still drained."

Sandra giggled. "Well, we're BFF when it comes to shopping. We went to two malls and it was heaven. Let me go before I make us late for our reservation. I need at least an hour to transform into sexy and flirtatious."

She reached for him, drawing him to her, their bodies touching.

"Now if you do that, we just may not get to dinner."

"Oh, we will, but we may not need to stay for dessert," she replied, slipping out of his grasp and stepping away. She waved goodbye and headed inside, leaving him looking on hungrily.

Dessert indeed!

He'd lost all desire for food. The only thing that could satisfy his hunger right now was Sandra.

What was happening to him? To them?

In a short space of time, their relationship had moved from hesitant, reluctant foreplay to teasing lovers. But he loved the change—the light, flirtatious, casual relationship they had. He enjoyed teasing her as he'd just done. He liked this.

He glanced down at his watch. It was just after five. He'd go rest while she got ready.

Today had been a hard day at work. He'd had a six-hour surgery to remove a brain tumor. His body and fingers were tired and had been pushed to the limit. But he'd been successful, and the patient would be all right.

He loved healing, and that's where the satisfaction from his job came. It was not the position or the praise that came from the medical community. For a while he'd become distracted by his father's insistence that he be the best. Now he realized that that wasn't the important thing. He gave people a chance to live again. That was what mattered.

Stretching out on the bed, he closed his eyes, but opened them immediately when the phone rang.

His mother's voice came over the phone.

"Troy, this is your mother."

"Yes, Mom," he replied, laughter in his voice. After all these years, his mother still greeted individuals over the phone like that.

"I haven't heard from you in ages. And you haven't come over for dinner yet. Is your girlfriend still staying there? I can't believe you haven't brought her over."

"Mom, you're exaggerating. I spoke to you two days ago, remember? And Sandra isn't my girlfriend. She's just a friend of Shayne and Carla's who's staying here because the kids have chicken pox. She's soon going back to the U.S."

"Well, that's not what I heard."

"What did you hear? And from whom?"

"You know that darling boy, George. I went to him this morning to take care of a legal matter and he told me all about you and Sandra. I remember her from the wedding. She's a lovely girl. I always told your father you have good taste."

"Mom, George was only pulling your leg. Sandra's just a good friend."

"Troy Whitehall. Don't you dare lie to your mother! Are you sleeping with her?"

"Mom, what kind of question are you asking me?"

"The kind of question that a mother can ask and one that demands an answer. Are you sleeping with her?"

He was about to tell her it was none of her business, but he decided against it.

"Yes," he said softly, somehow hoping she wouldn't hear.

"Good, I was starting to get worried that you didn't want to get married. You're almost forty and still haven't brought a young lady for me to meet. Not that I'd have a problem if you were, but now I'm getting old I want some grandchildren to spoil. Make sure you do this the right way. Children need both a mother and a father. You like Sandra, make sure you put a ring on her finger before someone else does."

"Yes, Mom."

"And let me say one thing. I didn't raise you to be playing around and having casual sex. You don't hurt that young lady. She's a sweet child. If you're only about that, then you leave her alone."

"I promise, Mom."

"Good, I don't want no son who's a good-for-nothing playa. So when is your girlfriend going back to the U.S?"

"In about a week or so."

"So you're going to invite her to stay the rest of the time there. Makes sense to me if she's sleeping in your bed. You won't have to be driving over to Shayne's house all hours of the morning to take her back."

The thought had crossed his mind, and he did plan to ask her at dinner.

"Yes, Mom, I'm taking her out to dinner tonight and planned on asking her."

"Good, always knew you had common sense along with that academic brain of yours."

"Thanks, Mom. I got both from you."

"You're trying to be sarcastic with me, son? I'll come over there and put a whupping on you." He could hear the laughter in her voice.

"Love you, Mom, but I need to go get ready for dinner."

"Yes, and wear that blue shirt I gave you at Christmas. Make that lady proud to be out with you."

"Thanks, Mom. Bye."

"Oh, and remember to call and let me know when you're bringing Sandra to lunch or dinner. She and I have a lot to talk about."

Before he could respond, she'd put the phone down. He laughed. His mother was a trip.

He walked over to the closet and looked for the blue shirt his mother had mentioned. With black trousers, he knew he'd look his best.

A long shower later, he dressed and looked at the clock. Twenty minutes before they would leave. Hopefully, Sandra would soon be ready.

He walked downstairs and grabbed the book he was currently reading. He was absorbed in the tale of a psychotic serial killer when Sandra walked into the room.

The book dropped from his lap.

She was stunning. She was gorgeous.

She wore a classy, sexy red number that stopped just above her knees. It fit her closely, emphasizing her generous curves and her firm breasts. His hands itched to touch her, but he clenched them.

She'd put her hair up into something, he wasn't sure what it was, but it made her look sexy and sophisticated. Her face was perfectly made up, with shades that complemented her complexion. Her eyes seemed large and more revealing, and he noticed the flash of desire as she looked at him.

He stood, forcing himself under control. He had to focus on dinner or they wouldn't leave home. He wanted to do something romantic, make Sandra feel special.

"You look lovely," he said.

"And you look like a gentleman."

"See, I can dress up when I need to. I don't wear scrubs all the time."

"Okay, let's stop all the admiration. I'm looking forward to eating out."

"So am I," he said, his voice strained and deep.

"Aren't you always? It's the maid's day off and I didn't feel like cooking, so your invitation was a blessing."

"Oh, so that's why you agreed to go out with me," he teased.

"Definitely, Dr. Whitehall. What other reason could I have for going with you?" she replied, smiling.

They reached the car, and he moved to the passenger side to open the door for her, waiting until she was seated and comfortable before closing it.

He walked around to the driver's side, slipped into the seat and started the engine, accelerating quickly.

"I'm going to remember that statement later," he finally responded, laughter in his voice.

"I love a man who enjoys a challenge."

He smiled again. Tonight was going to be interesting.

They were silent for the rest of the drive, listening

to the strains of local music, reggae soca, a fusion of reggae and calypso.

They traveled along the ABC Highway, leaving it at the Dover roundabout, and then went along the south coast until they reached Bay Street and turned onto Aquatic Gap, which led to the Hilton Hotel. Before reaching the hotel, Troy pulled into the parking lot of his place for eating out, the Brown Sugar Restaurant, a popular dining spot for both locals and visitors.

Troy knew it was the perfect place for romance. Tonight, he had all intentions of wining, dining and romancing her. He wanted to treat her like a lady.

Strangely enough, Sandra had never been to the Brown Sugar Restaurant despite its reputation for great local food.

Nestled in a cozy tropical setting, the restaurant's ambience was perfect for romance.

A single steel-pan player provided the soothing rhythms of the island, creating the perfect atmosphere for lovers.

A hostess led them to their table amidst the tropical foliage that was so much a part of the place's ambience.

She fell in love with the restaurant immediately. She loved its vivid shades of green, which gave a feeling of richness. Part of the restaurant's charm lay in the lush fern-filled patios. Cascading water gardens, together with the chirping of tree frogs, created a mood that was not only serene but romantic. Flickering candles provided the only light.

Leaving them to browse the menu, the waitress, with

a broad smile on her face, promised to return when they were ready. The waitresses' costumes were in keeping with the restaurant's cultural theme.

Sandra chose the stuffed roast pork Caribe, a dish of lean Barbados pork with a plantain-and-bacon stuffing, served with traditional Bajan pan gravy, while Troy chose the plantain-crusted mahi-mahi dolphin, a filet of mahi-mahi coated with a blend of plantain chips and cornmeal, sautéed and served with a plantain-and-pineapple chutney.

When the waitress returned with their drinks, Troy placed their orders. While waiting on their meals, they sipped slowly at the exotic drinks, embracing the mood of their surroundings.

"I love this place. Thanks for bringing me here."

"I always enjoy the food. I don't get here often for dinner, but the lunchtime buffet is fabulous."

"I'd love to come back during the day. I must tell Tamara and Carla so we can have a girls' outing here before I return to Atlanta," she said. She looked him in the eyes. "Do you bring all your girlfriends here?" she asked, her curiosity getting the better of her.

"In fact, I never have. I'm not one for dinner dates. It's has always been…" He stopped. "Let's just say, I've never been out with anyone whom I wanted to bring here."

She felt herself blush, and an unexpected wave of happiness rushed through her body.

"I've never thought anyone was special enough to bring here before. The restaurant at night is for lovers."

His response came as a dare, as if he were challenging her to deny his role in her life.

"Then I feel honored to be the first to come here with you."

"I assure you, I brought you here because I wanted to spend time with you. I'm not expecting dessert after."

"I'll always remember this. Of course, I'm going to make sure I recommend this place to clients, especially the couples, coming here on holiday."

He was about to say something when the waitress returned with their meals.

While the waitress placed their food on the table, Sandra took the time to look at Troy. There was something different about him tonight. A softness and gentleness she didn't often expect from him. She couldn't remember ever seeing this side of him.

But this Troy could grow on her. He not only seemed gentler but he was more relaxed, as if the job was not at the forefront of his mind.

As soon as the waitress told them to enjoy their meal, Sandra lifted the knife and fork up and took the first bite of the tropical fare.

The delicious, savory food exploded on her taste buds, until she almost groaned with the sensuous pleasure.

"This is so good," she said, before she put the second forkful in her mouth.

Troy, too, seemed focused on the meal and she was glad he didn't interrupt her culinary experiences with idle chitchat. There would be time for that later.

When she was done, she closed her eyes and sat back in the chair.

"I can see that you really enjoyed that," he observed.

She opened her eyes. He, too, had finished.

"That was what I'd call a culinary experience. The food was sumptuous. Just perfect."

The waitress walked over.

"I hope you are enjoying your meal," she said. "Would you like dessert or would you prefer coffee or tea?" she asked. "Maybe a glass of wine?"

"Since it is dessert," Sandra said, glancing at the menu, "I'm going to have dessert. Now let me see. I'd love some of the white chocolate cheesecake, topped with the mango coulis and toasted coconut. I know it sounds sinful, but I can't help but give in to the temptation."

"I'm like you, I must have my dessert," Troy agreed. "Blame it on my sweet tooth. I'm going to have the warm paw-paw pie with the vanilla ice cream."

"Good choices," the waitress said. "I'll be right back."

Five minutes later, she was back, the sweet concoctions in hand.

Later, Sandra watched as Troy held his stomach and sighed with satisfaction.

"I can't eat another mouthful. I won't be able to eat for at least two days, I feel so full," he said.

"I know how you feel, but I enjoyed every bit of the meal."

"Let's go down to the beach and walk it off." He beckoned the waitress over. She appeared and handed him the bill, which he paid by credit card and then stood to leave, waiting for her to stand.

When they left the restaurant, they turned left and walked the short distance to the beach.

The night was cool, the moon was almost full, its rays providing the light needed to see ahead of them. Stars sparkled in the sky like tiny diamonds, tempting Sandra to stretch her hands up and capture their beauty.

In the distance, Sandra could hear the sea, its music soothing and its rhythm in tune with her mood. She felt happy and reflective. They walked, absorbing the night sounds, afraid that if they talked, the mood would somehow be broken.

When they reached the sand, she bent and took her shoes off. The cool sand crunched under her feet, its texture soft and grainy.

She laughed, finally breaking the silence, the sound one of total happiness.

"Take your shoes off," she commanded.

He looked at her as if she'd gone mad, but eventually bent and slipped them off, holding them in his hands.

"Doesn't it feel wonderful? I feel like a kid. The water must be wonderful this time of night."

"I'm sure it is, but don't you dare get any ideas," he cautioned.

"No, no. I didn't mean for us to swim. This beach is a bit too busy for that," she responded, acknowledging another couple walking ahead of them, and a group with a bonfire farther down the beach.

Minutes later they stopped, resting under the canopy

of an almond tree. As they stood looking out to sea, Troy turned her to face him.

She sighed in anticipation, waiting for him to kiss her, her body feeling all tingly and warm. His lips touched her gently, softly.

His hand rested at the back of her head, giving him access to her throat.

Sandra placed her hand on the back of his head, drawing him closer.

The kiss was magic.

Then the cell in her bag began to ring. He moved away.

"No, we don't have to stop," she said.

"It may be important."

The ringing stopped, but she reached into her bag reluctantly, glancing at the number that had registered.

"I'm not sure who…" she said. Before she could finish her statement, the phone rang again.

This time she answered it. A strange voice came over the line, the message direct and clear.

She flicked the phone shut and stood quietly.

"What's wrong?" he asked.

When she answered her voice sounded strained and hollow.

"It's my father. He's in the hospital. He's had a very serious stroke."

As she said the words, the tears came, and he pulled her back to him, holding her as she shivered with the fear of what could happen.

# *Chapter 11*

Troy wondered if Sandra was asleep. The moment they'd stepped into the house, she had excused herself and gone up to her room. An hour later, she'd still not reappeared. He felt hopeless, a feeling he rarely experienced.

When he'd tried to follow her upstairs, she'd told him she wanted to be alone and he'd stepped back as if she'd slapped him in his face. He had wanted to offer her comfort, but she'd refused. Maybe she needed to be alone to deal with her conflicting feelings for her father. He should be able to understand, but it did not stop the pain he felt inside for her.

He still wasn't sure about his place in her life.

He had to go to her, to make sure she was all right.

If she asked him to leave, he would, but for now he had to see her.

He climbed up the stairs, taking two steps at a time. When he reached her room, he knocked, but there was no answer.

He knocked again, but still no answer. He pushed the door gently.

Her clothes lay on the floor, and she lay on the bed curled like a comma. He stood by the bed looking down at her. She was fast asleep, but she'd been crying. The remnants of tears still stained her cheeks.

As if realizing someone was there, she woke, her eyes opening slowly, at first confused until she realized it was him.

"I'm sorry," she said. "I didn't mean to push you away." Seeing her distress almost broke his heart.

"I understand," he replied. "I didn't like it, but I understand."

"Come lie next to me. Hold me."

He didn't hesitate. He parted the covers and slipped between them, placed his arms around her, her back against his chest. For a while, they were silent. He knew that she had something to say, but he waited, wanting her to say what she had to when she was ready.

When she spoke it was in a soft, sad voice.

"I want to hate him. I thought I hated him, but all I feel right now is pain. He killed my mother, and for years I wanted nothing to do with him. He tried to contact me on several occasions, and I never returned his calls."

"You can't blame yourself for that. He made his choice when he walked out on you and your mother."

"Maybe that's so. I don't know what to do. I don't know if I should go and see him. The doctor who called said he's really bad. It's the second stroke he has had. He doesn't have anyone. The doctor says he has tried to reach his ex-wife, but no luck. I didn't know he wasn't married anymore. What if he dies? I'm not sure I want him to die alone. The doctor told me I need to come and soon."

"You can try to get on a flight tomorrow or the next day."

"How do you know I'm going to go?"

"I know you. However you feel about your dad, I know you, you'll go."

"I'll go, but I don't want to go on my own. I can't ask Carla to go with me. The kids are now recovering from illness and Tamara has her own kids and business."

"I can go with you."

She laughed. "I won't ask you to do that. You have patients to worry about. It'll be too much of an imposition."

"I'm serious, it won't be a problem. My holiday is long overdue, and any of the doctors in my department can take care of anything major. I can be reached by phone. It's just four hours from here to the U.S."

"You're sure about this?" she asked.

"Yes, I'm sure. I don't want you to be alone at this time."

"Thanks. I don't think I could have dealt with this on my own."

"Well, you get some sleep. I'll call the airport as soon as I get up in the morning to check the flights for tomorrow. If we don't get a direct flight, we may be able to go through Puerto Rico. An extra hour or so, but we'll still get there."

"Thanks," she said again.

He kissed her on her forehead as her eyes closed.

She was soon asleep.

When she woke in the morning, Troy was gone. A moment of panic unsettled her, but she immediately realized she was being paranoid. He was probably downstairs making breakfast. And then she remembered. The phone calls...her father.

She jumped from the bed, racing to the bathroom where she quickly brushed the teeth and threw on a T-shirt and shorts.

She didn't find Troy in the kitchen and moved quickly to his office.

He was there and looked up when she entered.

"How are you this morning?" he asked.

She smiled, a smile that she didn't feel, but she was glad to see him.

She raced over to him and put her arms around him.

"Thank you. I don't know what I'd have done without you."

"It's fine. You'll be glad to know that I got us tickets for today. The flight leaves at 3:30. I've purchased the tickets online, so we just have to get to the airport. I'll drive and leave the car there. George will pick it up."

"Thanks. I don't know what to say."

"Just go to the kitchen and have the breakfast that's in the microwave. And call Carla and let her know. I'll be gone for an hour. I've already spoken to my boss and everything will be fine. Just a little while ago he told me I needed to get some rest. He'll be glad I'm taking his advice."

"I feel so bad about putting you through so much trouble."

"Trouble? What are friends for? Let's not hear that kind of talk anymore. Go get your breakfast. I'm going to leave in a few minutes."

He bent and kissed her on the lips, awakening her weary body. Even now she wanted him, but she needed to focus on what was ahead.

Leaving him on the computer, she headed to the kitchen and, as he'd said, found her breakfast in the microwave. She warmed it up, checking to see that coffee had been made and turning the coffeemaker on to heat it up. She was surprised at her appetite when she ate all of what Troy had prepared.

She headed back to the bedroom to pack, but before she did, she picked the phone up. Carla answered on the second ring.

"Morning, Sandra. I'm not accustomed to hearing you so early in the morning."

"I have to go back to Atlanta."

"So soon. Is something wrong?"

"It's my dad. He's had a stroke." Her voice cracked, but she forced herself not to cry. She didn't want Carla to be worried. "I was told that it's his second one. The doctor doesn't think he has long to live."

"I'm sorry to hear. When do you leave?"

"Today. Troy got us a flight that leaves at 3:30."

"Us?" Carla asked.

"Yes, he's going with me."

"Now that's nice to hear. Unfortunately, it's probably not appropriate to ask you for all the juicy details since your dad is not well, but I can assume that everything is going well with the two of you?"

"I think so. It's getting…much better."

"That's good. I love both of you and want to see you happy."

"Maybe, but we're taking things one day at a time. Don't want to rush into anything I'd regret later."

"That's the mature way to do things. Make sure you call us when you get home. Thanks again for taking care of the kids while we were on holiday. I really appreciate it."

"That's what godparents are there for. I really enjoyed being with them."

"That doesn't mean I can't say thanks. And I know that my kids are a handful."

"No, they aren't. They are just kids."

"I love you, BFF."

Sandra laughed. "Love you, too."

She put the phone down, fighting the sting of tears. She loved Carla like a sister. They'd always been close. From the day they'd sat across from each other in the school's cafeteria and she'd said to Carla, "I'll give you half of my pizza if you give me half of your burger."

They'd smiled at each other and for years had been inseparable until Carla had gotten married.

But they were still BFF.

She did know one thing. She wanted what Carla had. She wanted it all. The white wedding dress, the honeymoon, the picket fence and wonderful, wonderful babies.

But she'd deal with that when this crisis was over. For now she had to deal with confronting her father.

But the initial trepidation was gone. She knew Troy would be there with her, and knowing that made her feel relieved and safe.

The airplane lifted off the tarmac at the scheduled time. Both she and Troy slept most of the flight with an interruption when they were offered an in-flight meal.

She'd never traveled first-class before, but she could easily get accustomed to it. She could endure being called a snob just for the VIP treatment and the oh-so-comfortable seats.

When the American Airline flight touched down at Hartsfield-Jackson Atlanta International Airport four hours later, she was more than tired. All she wanted to do was sleep. Tomorrow, they'd go to the hospital first thing in the morning. Tonight, a call to the hospital should be enough.

When they arrived at her brownstone in the quiet gated community where she lived, the sun had already set.

Using her security pass, they entered and made their way along the winding driveway before stopping in a parking lot in front of a row of very eclectic town houses.

She parked quickly, aware that she was not only tired but hungry.

Thank God, she'd had the good sense to stop and purchase Chinese food on the way home.

"You have a beautiful home. Must have cost a bundle," he observed.

"It was a bit more than I anticipated, but when my mother died she left me quite comfortable. I was able to buy Carla's half of the business, so you could say I'm comfortable."

"Comfortable? You're way rich! I couldn't afford to live here."

"Troy, in Barbados, you would definitely be considered well-off. And your home is not much smaller than mine."

"Okay, you've made your point."

"Come, let's go in. It's cool outside, and I'm tired and hungry. I want to give the hospital a call, too. Find out how my dad's doing."

While she made a call to the hospital, Troy took the luggage to the rooms she'd indicated and searched in his suitcase to find a pair of shorts. He usually slept in the nude but didn't think it would be a sensible thing to do, since his control around her was nonexistent. He didn't want her feeling, in her time of crisis, that all he wanted to do was make love to her.

He was horrible, but he couldn't help it. He couldn't remember ever feeling like this, even in his teenage years.

He stripped and headed into the bathroom. Maybe he'd take his bath and be done before she came.

There were no towels on the rack so he searched the few cupboards before he found a stack of towels. He chose a plain-colored one; the others were too floral. He searched and found an unopened toothbrush. He hadn't even thought about those things.

He placed his clothes in the basket and stepped into the shower. At the same time he heard footsteps. Sandra appeared at the door, her clothes already off.

"I don't believe you were planning to shower without me," she chided.

"Sorry, I wasn't sure how soon you'd be up. But I'd be delighted if you joined me," he replied.

She stepped in at his urging, immediately putting her hands around him.

"Thanks," she said.

"For?" he asked.

"For being there for me," she said.

"It's the least I could do. We may have got off to a rocky start, but you're my friend."

"Only your friend?"

"And lover, if you'd have me," he said.

"I didn't know that I had to say it out loud," she replied.

"I'm a man who never takes things for granted."

"Then yes, friend and lover."

"And what after that?" he asked.

"I could say many things, but I'm comfortable with the way things are."

"And how is that?"

"That we be friends and lovers and let things develop from there. See where it goes. I could say yes, we'll be friends and lovers and then you propose to me and we live happily ever after. The reality is that we don't know each other. We are getting to know each other and maybe that's the way things should be. We both have our feelings and both of us are not ready to put them into words because we're scared. Because we don't want to presume the possibilities."

"That's true," he agreed. "As you say, let's get to know each other. Be friends and lovers. When it's time to take the next step, we'll know."

"Sounds good to me," she replied. "Right now, I want to take a shower, make love to you and then have a good night's sleep."

"Maybe we should make love, take a shower and then sleep."

"Sounds like a plan to me," she replied.

And he proceeded to oblige her, there in the shower, the water trickling around them, hearts pounding, until they reached the peak of the mountain of pleasure. They basked in the sunlight of desire and they both cried out in ecstasy, their souls bared and exposed before each other.

A quick shower and they were soon fast asleep in each other's arms.

The next morning, they arrived at the hospital just after 10:00 a.m. Sandra had hoped to get there before, but they'd awakened later than expected, a combination of jet lag and passionate lovemaking.

When they reached the nurses' station and made an inquiry, they were directed to the ward where her father was.

Outside, she paused and turned to Troy.

"Just give me a few minutes. I need to do this on my own."

"I understand, honey," he replied, bending to kiss her lightly on the lips.

"Thank you," she said, returning the kiss and not wanting it to stop.

Reluctantly, she stepped back and turned, pushing the door of the room.

When she stepped inside, it took her a while to adjust to the dim light.

She walked over to the bed. He was sleeping, an uncomfortable sleep. His breaths came in strained, harsh spasms. Machines she didn't know, but had seen on TV, seemed to protrude from every part of his body.

Tears sprang to her eyes. Was this the man who'd given her life? She couldn't believe it. He was a frail manifestation of his former self. Her father had been handsome, strong and brawny. She remembered her friends going crazy about him when she was in high school.

The man lying before her bore those features no more. His skin was pale, not the rich burnished color she remembered. His hair was almost completely gone. He was a barely living skeleton.

A wave of sadness washed over her. Though a part of her hated him for what he'd done to her mother, she still remembered times she'd spent with him. Images of him flashed in her mind—reading to her, dancing with her and spinning her round and round until they tumbled onto the couch, peals of laughter filling the house.

"Dad," she said softly.

At first there was no response, but when she spoke his name again, his eyes opened slowly.

Immediately, his eyes widened and tears slowly pooled there. A pain like none she'd ever experienced before ripped at her heart. Hatred she'd carried for years dissipated.

She reached out to hold his hand, its coldness startling her. Gently, she squeezed it.

His mouth opened slowly, as pain etched his face.

He mumbled something, but she did not hear clearly.

He tried again, so she bent her torso, positioning her face near to his mouth. He mumbled something, which she did not hear, but instinct told her he'd asked for forgiveness.

"I forgive you," she said.

Tears trickled down his cheeks and he closed his eyes again. The effort to talk had tired him. In a while, he was asleep, his hand still holding hers.

When Troy entered the room almost thirty minutes later, he found her there, still holding her father's hand.

She looked so sad and hurt that he wasn't sure what to do or say. This love thing was difficult to understand. He knew that he didn't want to see her hurting and that he'd do anything to help her through this crisis.

She looked at him when he entered, her eyes big and

sad, and he felt an ache like none he'd ever experienced before.

Was this how it was going to be? It scared him, made him feel weak and helpless, and he wasn't sure if he liked feeling like this.

But he didn't feel like running. He wanted to be here for her. Nothing else mattered.

He walked over to her, watching as she rose, the expression on her face one of confusion. But she quickly pulled herself together, her strong, confident persona returning.

"He's gone back to sleep. His body needs the rest. I need to find the doctor. I need to know..." She stopped. He could tell she was battling for her composure.

"That's a good idea," he replied, reaching for her hand.

She followed his lead, exiting the room and headed back to the nurses' station.

Upon their request, the nurse made a quick phone call.

"Dr. Chandler is expecting you," she said, after hanging up the phone. "Just walk along the corridor, make a left turn. It's the third door on the right. His name is on the door, so it shouldn't be difficult to find."

"Thank you," Sandra replied.

Following the instructions, they found the doctor's room and knocked.

A deep voice said, "Come in."

Troy did not move when she pushed the door open. She turned around and said, "Come inside with me."

"Are you sure?" he asked.

"I'm sure," she replied.

He followed her in, coming to stop before a large desk and a small man.

The man sitting at the desk seemed so unlike a doctor, that Sandra at first felt skeptical about his ability, but dismissed the feeling. She'd reserve her judgment until later.

She and Troy sat when Dr. Chandler indicated two chairs before him.

"It's nice to meet you both. I'm sorry we had to meet under these circumstances," Dr. Chandler said pleasantly.

"Thank you, Dr. Chandler," Sandra responded.

"I think it better if I be as honest as possible with you. Your father has had a series of strokes during the past two years. This one is the worst one. Along with that, he's been diagnosed with cancer. We'd originally given him six months to live. That was four months ago. The complications from his hypertension have not made it any easier. Along with that, I think your father has given up on life. His last words to me were that he had nothing to live for."

Shame washed over her and Troy's discomfort increased. The doctor's words had upset her. Troy squeezed her hand, offering reassurance.

"No need to worry. I make no judgment about your relationship with your father. He explained the situation to me and wanted me to tell you that he isn't angry with you for not coming to see him. All that has happened to him is his entire fault."

"And what about his wife?" she asked, curiosity getting the better of her.

"Oh, they were divorced several years ago. I can't give you the details. His lawyer will be contacting you soon."

"I'll make sure that everything is taken care of. Is there anything that can be done?" she asked.

"No, I know your father just wants to die in peace. The only thing that was important to him was that you forgive him."

She nodded, unable to speak, the full weight of what was happening almost physically pressing her down.

She stood quickly, wanting to get out of the room. Troy stood, too, resting a hand lightly on her arm. His warmth offered her the reassurance she needed. She drew strength from his touch.

"Thank you for your time, Dr. Chandler," Troy said, taking control. "We'll be back later this afternoon to see Mr. Walters again."

Taking Sandra's hand, he led her out of the room. Outside, she leaned against him, her arms wrapped around his waist.

Again, she wondered how she'd ever repay him for what he offered.

For a while they stood there, holding each other.

Despite all that was happening, Sandra felt safe.

Later that evening, before they could return to the hospital for their planned visit, they received a call from Dr. Chandler. Her father had passed away.

This time Sandra did not cry. Instead, while Troy

held her in his arms, she talked about her dad and all the good things she remembered about him.

On reflection, she realized he'd been the one to instill in her a love for traveling. She remembered the trips he'd taken them on, to New York's Broadway and her most favorite place, New Orleans.

The rest of the day, passed in a blurred haze. As the doctor had said, her father had made all the arrangements, but she spent the time making sure that all his wishes were being carried out.

By the time they reached home, just after the sun had set, she felt drained of what little energy she had left. When they entered the house, she went straight to her bedroom and took a shower. Troy had told her he'd order in dinner. She didn't care much about food, but she needed to eat. The next few days were going to be difficult.

After her shower, she lay on the bed and, closing her eyes, tried to fall asleep.

When Troy entered the bedroom an hour later, Sandra was still sleeping. While she slept, he'd taken a quick shower and remained downstairs until the Chinese food arrived.

His stomach grumbled. He carried the tiny boxes, a carton of fruit juice and two glasses.

In the room, he placed dinner on the table next to the bed and gently shook her.

She slowly came awake.

"What's wrong?" she said.

"I thought we could have a picnic now that dinner

has arrived. We'll have apple pie and ice-cream a little later. I have a copy of *Funny Lady* that I found in the DVDs."

"Here? We're going to have a picnic here in my bed?" she asked, as if she thought he was going crazy.

"Of course. With Chinese food. You're scared of being adventurous?" he teased. "I brought a big plastic tablecloth and if you'd remove yourself from the bed for a bit so I can spread it, I can set up our picnic goodies. Plus, we don't have any ants to worry about."

She laughed, a joyous, delightful sound that made his heart feel like soaring. He'd not heard her laugh or smile since she'd received the news about her father.

"I'm going to have to admit how hungry I am. I haven't really felt like eating until I smelled that mouth-watering sweet-and-sour chicken."

"Good, don't want you looking all skinny and frail. You're slim as it is. I love Chinese food and like you always say, 'I could eat a horse.'"

"No need to worry. The amount that came is enough to feed us for a few days," he commented.

"Good. For some reason, I'm really hungry."

When he was done putting everything on the bed, he placed a movie in the DVD player and turned the television on. The movie was one of her favorites; Barbara Streisand's *Funny Lady*. He'd chosen it deliberately. He wanted to lift her sadness. His heart ached. He didn't like her being sad.

Two hours later, he turned the TV off and turned to her. "Ready for dessert?" he asked.

She nodded and said, "There's a box of my favorite

Sara Lee apple pie in the refrigerator, as well as a few containers of Häagen-Dazs ice cream," she replied. "Bring two scoops of the pineapple coconut."

"Why don't I bring the whole container and we'll eat out of it," he said, a broad smile on his face. He had something in mind.

"Okay, I'll leave everything in your capable hands."

When he left the room, she rested her head on the pillow. For a while, she'd been able to forget her father. She couldn't believe he was dead. He'd always been there in the back of her mind.

There was a part of her that regretted that she'd not been there for him in his last days. The man had deteriorated from one of the best surgeons she'd known to a man who'd almost died alone. She wondered what had happened to his young wife. She suspected that "Silicone Breasts" had moved on.

The door opened and Troy stepped inside carrying two bowls. He sat on the bed and handed her one of them. Inside was the most sinful-looking concoction, and her mouth immediately began to water.

Instead of allowing her to eat from her bowl, he lifted a spoonful to her mouth. She allowed him access, the chilly sweetness assaulting her taste buds. *It was so good.*

She returned the favor, feeding him a brimming spoonful.

Their eyes locked, each seeing the passion flaming inside. He reached for her bowl, placing both on the side table, and moved closer to her. He pulled her to him, raising her hands above her head to slip her blouse off. She raised her torso, allowing him to pull her shorts off.

When he was done, he stood, making light work of his own clothing until he stood looking down at her, his desire evident.

He crawled onto the bed, his body above her. She'd waited for this for a long time. There was part of her that felt that with her father's death, she should be focused on other things. But tonight, she wanted Troy. She wanted to make love to him.

During the night, Troy woke. Sandra's head lay against his chest. He nuzzled her, inhaling the flowery scent of the bath gel she used. They'd made love into the early hours of the morning and then again when they'd taken a shower.

Outside, the sky was a pale dull gray, the sun forcing its way from below the horizon. It would soon be morning.

He felt good waking with her next to him.

He loved her.

The thought came unexpectedly, but a rush of happiness filled him.

He'd felt it for some time, but he'd not had the courage to admit it. Now he needed to say it. To say it now would determine the direction of his life.

He had come to realize something. He wanted what Shayne and Russell had. He wanted to wake up each morning and find this wonderful, sensitive, strong woman sleeping next to him. He lowered his head, placing a soft kiss on her forehead.

She turned in his arms, her breasts brushing across his chest.

Damn, he loved this woman.

He wanted to make her life a happy one. He wanted to give her beautiful babies that looked like a combination of the best of each of them.

He knew now what made life important. Yes, it was going after your dreams, but finding someone to share and embrace those dreams with you made it even better.

He knew that her dislike for doctors would have to change, but hoped that that uncertainty would not remain. He'd have to prove to her that all doctors were not like her father.

He had a good example and in time, Sandra would see that his parents were happy and loved each other. Maybe seeing true love would have a positive impact on her.

When Sandra awoke in the morning, it was to silence. For a moment she panicked, but knew there was no reason for her to be scared. Knowing Troy, he was likely in the kitchen making breakfast.

She quickly rose from the bed and slipped her robe on. She was hungry. Sex always made her hungry. Especially sex like the sex she shared with Troy.

Even now as she thought about their lovemaking last night, she longed to feel him inside her again. She'd only have him all tired out, and the next few days of preparing for her father's funeral needed all the energy she could muster.

As she was about to step out the door, it opened and Troy entered, not a stitch on.

He slowly and seductively walked over to her.

"So what do you think? Think I'm sexy?"

"More than sexy," she replied, crooking a finger at him seductively. He complied, joining her on the bed and wrapping his arms around her. She resisted playfully, punching him gently in the stomach.

For a few minutes they wrestled and tossed on the bed, until, exhausted she lay under him, their faces inches apart.

She lay quietly, aware of his erection against her leg. She wanted him to make love to her again, but the slight soreness between her legs made her speak cautiously.

"I think we may need to take a bit of a rest."

Troy shifted immediately.

"Did I hurt you?" he asked, concern in his voice.

"No, but I do feel a bit…"

"Sore," he continued. "I'm so sorry. We did it a bit too much."

"No, it's okay. I wanted you each time. I'm not some fragile little Barbie, but yes, we need to take a break."

"That's fine with me. My back was about to give out," he admitted. "Seems I'm not as young as I used to be. I'm probably going to have all my muscles hurting tomorrow. But no worry, we have a lifetime ahead of us." He stopped, realizing what he'd said. Under him, her heart and breathing stopped. What was he saying?

"I was going to wait until all of this was over. Your father's funeral."

She felt the sting of tears. No, no, she was not going to cry.

"I remember the first time I met you. I wanted you. You were the most beautiful woman I'd ever seen. And then we made love and I was in heaven, until I realized how much you hated the thought of marrying a doctor."

"I'm sorry. I know now my feelings are irrational," she said.

"Then I thought it would never be," Troy continued. "But at that time, I was so focused on my work and being the best neurosurgeon I could be. I had no intentions of ever getting married. I planned on devoting my life to my career."

She listened intently. She knew he had something else to say.

"But you saved me. Saved me with your kisses and your embrace. You made me realize I wanted more out of life than my dedication to my profession and my need to be the best. I want and need you. I can't imagine living my life without you. I love you."

She smiled. He was so sweet.

"It's fine, Troy. I love you, too. Have always loved you. Of course, I'd been so focused on what my father did to us, I didn't allow myself to open to you, but over time, I realized what a special man you are. You touch so many people's lives with the work that you do."

He smiled, nodding in response.

"So my healer, my lover, my friend. I love you more than life itself," she said.

"So will you marry me, Sandra Walters?" he asked, his eyes filled with love.

"Of course I will," she replied, squealing and wrapping her hands around him.

"Good, now I can go back to sleep and try to recover before we make love again."

He laughed, a sound that echoed around the room.

She closed her eyes, drawing closer to him.

She loved his laughter and planned on waking to it each morning for the rest of her life.

The next few days were going to be sad ones, but in the midst of the sadness, hope shone brightly like the sun in summer. She'd lost her father, but she'd found the most important thing.

She'd found love.

# *Epilogue*

Troy sat next to his wife at the head wedding table. In a few hours, he would be starting his life with her. To say she looked beautiful was an understatement. She was the most beautiful woman sitting under the large tent where the reception was being kept.

When he'd asked Shayne if he could have his wedding and reception on the grounds of the plantation, Shayne had immediately agreed.

In the three months that followed his proposal to Sandra, Carla, Tamara and Tori had taken charge of planning the grandest wedding the island had ever seen.

The result had been spectacular. The plantation gardens had been transformed into a place of glitz and glamour. Hundreds of candles flickered overhead, giving the illusion of a clear July night.

Sandra turned to him and whispered in his ear.

"So can we leave soon?" she asked.

"It's our wedding, honey. You can't go and leave your guests so soon," he replied, despite knowing that he also wanted to go.

"So when am I going to get dessert?" she purred, her tongue touching his earlobe for the briefest of seconds.

"You're hungry again," he replied, trying to ignore the shiver that raced through his body. "Didn't we have dessert during the dinner?" He tried to feign ignorance.

"But it was such a tiny amount," she whispered. He jumped. A finger trailed itself along his inner thigh. What was she trying to do to him? "I wanted something larger and more filling."

He laughed. "I actually have a wife who's a pervert in the making."

"Me? You're calling me a pervert? You were the one who wanted to sneak into my room last night. Just before the wedding."

"I do not see what's the big fuss. We made love only two days ago. Remember?" he said.

"Oh, I remember."

"You would remember. It *was* hot, wasn't it?" he commented.

"The best yet."

"You say that each time we make love."

"But it does get better each time. And you're good. I especially loved when you did that thing with your…"

"Mrs. Whitehall, can you please change the conversation? Or I'm going to have to forget we're sitting in front of three hundred of our best friends and ravish you right here."

"I agree, but don't put any other dessert on the menu tonight. I have a very special gift for you."

"Now that's one of the best things I've heard for the whole day. Hopefully, Carla will come and release us from our duties soon."

As if on cue, Carla stood, glancing at them. "It's time for the two honeymooners to get out of here."

She turned to the audience. "Ladies and gentlemen, I'm going to invite Dr. and Mrs. Whitehall to take the floor for the wedding dance. By special request, the song chosen is the current number-one single by Tori Matthews-Knight."

Cheers rang out, filling the plantation yard with excitement.

Troy stood, allowing his wife to stand before he led her to the center of the tent, which had been designated for dancing.

The couple was a picture of perfection, the two dancing gracefully, looking dreamily into each other's yes.

As they danced they whispered to each other.

Little did their guests know that the two were anticipating their dessert.

Two hours later, Sandra kissed her husband on his lips and spoke softly into his ear.

"Honey, that was incredible," Troy said. "I was inspired by that special gift. I must confess that I loved it."

"Oh, I knew you would," she said, running her hands along his chest.

"I'm hungry again," she said.

"For food?" Troy asked.

Sandra laughed. "Why would I want to eat when all I want to do is make love to my husband?"

"I'm not complaining. I'm a little tired, but I'm sure I can oblige my wife."

He turned over, facing her, hearing her breathing deepen.

He moved immediately to the core of her womanhood and with his tongue showed her how much he loved her.

On the other side of the island, Russell, George, Kyle and his adopted son, Jared, sat around a table, their laughter loud and raucous.

"Well, it's your turn next, George," Russell Knight said. "Shayne is gone and Troy is gone. That leaves you and Jared."

Jared laughed. "I assure you, I have a long time to go before I think about love. My research is taking up all of my time, and I have no time for love. I'm about ten years younger than all of you, so it's only fair that I let you older folk go first."

"Who are you calling old, boy? Girls your age want me. But I won't be getting married anytime soon, either, George."

"That's not what I've heard. Tamara keeps me informed about the heat in the courtroom," Kyle commented.

"What are you all talking about?" Jared asked.

"George is up against Rachel Davis."

"His former girlfriend?"

"Leave Rachel out of this!" George shouted. "There is nothing there."

"I say the gentleman protests too much. That courtroom must be steaming hot!" Kyle added, his laughter infectious.

"Can we please change the conversation, please? Jared, how's the work at college going?" George asked.

The conversation had changed, but in the minds of the four men who sat there was a question.

*Who's going to be next?*

\* \* \* \* \*

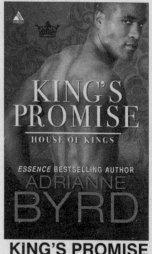

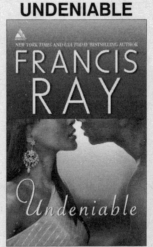